Rock ... paper ... scissors

For oldest brother Jared, losing the game is supposed to be a ticket out of the nightmare of family life.

Will, the winner, stays behind to take care of his younger siblings and his mom, Amy, as they search for their absent father, David, while staying in seedy motel rooms and living off money Amy gets from men "friends". Will has to be the husband, father, and brother, the Holy Trinity rolled into one package. In addition to reassuring the three youngest siblings, he works at keeping his beautiful sister Casey from picking up random boys, as she tries to deaden her pain with sex and cigarettes.

Then Will makes a momentous decision that breaks his family's heart but brings them back together after all else has failed.

Someday Never Comes is a gripping exploration of family ties and traumas, a coming-of-age story of struggles that reveal an intense and poignant love so powerful it leads one sibling to death, one to rejoining the family, and another to the possibility of a new life that breaks the inherited pattern of destruction.

"In this unflinching portrayal of a family in free fall, Rebecca Grove Munson writes with extraordinary sensitivity about the fragile architecture of stability and the mercilessness of its collapse. With precise, evocative prose, she captures the tender intimacies and brutal realities of life on society's margins, illuminating the fierce devotion that can bind a family together or tear it apart. Incandescent—and unforgettable."

"At turns tender and visceral, *Someday Never Comes* is a raw and unflinching portrait of a family in crisis. This is a darkly lyrical and moving work that packs a powerful punch."

Someday
Never
Comes

Someday Never Comes

Rebecca Grove Munson

A Labrador Book

Published by Labrador Books
St. Louis, Missouri

This book is a work of fiction. Any names, characters, companies, organizations, places, events, locales, and incidents are either used in a fictitious manner or are fictional. Any resemblance to actual persons, living or dead, actual companies or organizations, or actual events is purely coincidental.

For rights and permissions, please contact:
www.labradorbooks.com

ISBN: 978-0-9893615-5-2

Designed and typeset by Raspberry Creative Type,
Edinburgh

For family, friends, and supporters

And I still see him standin', tryin' to be a man.
I said, "Someday, you'll understand."

'Someday Never Comes',
Creedence Clearwater Revival

Contents

Casey 2000

Listening to the quiet, even breathing around me, I'm pretty sure they're all asleep. I swing my legs over the side of the bed and work my feet into the sandals waiting below, hoping not to shake the mattress too much.

"Casey?" a soft voice whispers in my ear.

Damn. Always one of them. I can never be quiet enough.

I turn. This time it's Sarah, hair tousled from sleep, looking younger than seven in Jen's Winnie-the-Pooh undershirt and a pair of ratty pink undies we should have thrown out long ago.

"Yeah, Sar?"

"Where are you going?"

"For a walk. Go to sleep."

I reach across the bed to tuck her back in. Jen lies next to her. Three kids in a double bed. It worked when we were little, but now it's crowded and hot and sticky, especially on a sweltering Louisiana night like this.

She's almost back to sleep as she murmurs, "Mama said not to leave tonight."

I get up slowly, hoping Jen won't wake. I glance at the next bed, where Mom is sound asleep, cradling Tommy to her. We wanted her to get her tubes tied after Sarah, but it took Tommy to convince her. Not that she doesn't love him. She loves all of us, or did at one time. Now I don't know if she even realizes who we are.

I slip into the bathroom, leaving it dark until I block the gap beneath the door with a towel. I flip the switch, and the light assaults my eyes. It comes from a row of unshaded bulbs above a tarnished mirror. The mirror itself hangs above a rickety, rust-stained sink. One of the taps is dripping, probably has been since the Seventies, and is wearing at the groove in the cracked porcelain beneath it.

I set to work unbuttoning the plaid shirt that I wore to bed. I cast it aside and readjust my tank top and cutoffs. The great thing about jeans is that they never show how old they are.

I pull a pair of earrings out of the pocket and stick them into a second set of holes. They're a little crooked since I did them myself, but it looks good.

No time for all my makeup, so I'll stick to essentials: blush, eyeliner, and lip gloss. I decide I'd better pull my hair back, because it's humid as a sauna outside. I grab my purse, making sure my cigarettes are where I left them—they're in a tampon case, so Will won't mess with them—and snap off the light.

Waiting a minute or so to let my eyes readjust to the darkness, I stand poised, with my hand on the doorknob. I move quietly through the doorway, past the double beds, and to the motel room door, passing an ancient a.c. wall unit, which is perspiring with the effort of relieving the summer heat.

As I turn the doorknob, I hear another voice say softly, "No, Casey."

I whirl around, opening the door and stepping out onto the shared porch and into the night. He follows me though. He always does.

"Will, go."

"Come back inside."

Every damn time. Why does he do it? We both know what's going to happen, so why does he keep fighting it? I try to lower my voice, keep it calm and reasonable, because it's always better when we don't have to fight.

"No, Will, we've been through this. I won't. Now go back to bed."

"No." Obstinate refusal. Classic Will.

He continues, his jaw set in a way that only I recognize as restraining tears. "I'm your older brother. I can't let you behave like this. Mom hates it." He pauses, then adds with defiance, "*Dad* would hate it!"

His eyes are flashing at me, bright-burning despite how dark they are. I falter slightly at this last unexpected attack.

"Yeah, well, Dad's gone, and Mom's no better."

My voice comes out harsh and grating, rubbed raw, the way I feel inside every time we check into another cheap motel room. He stiffens and turns away from me slightly.

Part of me wants to hold him, to comfort him like I would when we were younger, but he draws himself close in, and I know, somehow, that I cannot.

Almost instantly, my sympathy for him is consumed by anger, swelling and breaking in waves.

I challenge him, wrenching around his shoulder to get him to look at me.

"Did you *hear* me?"

He turns back to me, reaching out to seize my arm, then reconsiders. His voice is quiet and furious.

"Of course I did, but I didn't want to. You're acting so *selfish*, Casey. So goddamn selfish. Mom does what she has to for money. Do you like this motel room? Do you like it better than the pickup? Do you like being able to take a shower and have air conditioning? Then don't you say a word about what Mom does. At least she gets something for it, which is more than I can say for you."

His dark features look even more intense in the night. Some days he looks just like Dad, especially when he's as angry as he is now. I understand that he wants to protect me, but he doesn't have to. This is what I want.

He walks forward and leans against the railing, staring at the duck pond three floors down. His voice is soft and low now, his defeated voice. I know he'll let me go in a minute.

"Who is it tonight, Casey?"

"Paul. The boy at the counter who checked us in. He's waiting in the lobby."

He gets angry again, suddenly, not saying anything but twisting his face around so that I can see clearly what he's thinking.

I add, "And you're wrong. I do get something out of this, just not money." It sends him over the edge.

He spins me to him so that our faces are only inches apart and says furiously, "What could you possibly be getting from this? Leaving a boy or two everywhere you go, what good is that?"

"What good is moving from town to town? At least this way I get to forget my problems for a while. We shouldn't be going through these towns anyway. We should all be at home."

"You know Mom's just trying to find Dad. Maybe she will soon."

"I don't know how you're so dumb about this! Honestly, Will, you're so smart about everything else. It's been nearly four years, and we've been chasing him on those stupid letters to Grandma for a year-and-a-half. We don't deserve this. And it's illegal, keeping five kids out of school. We should live with Grandma, and if Mom wants to chase Dad, let her."

"You think I don't feel the same way? I'm missing all my opportunities in life just to ride around in a crowded pickup truck with four kids and a woman who's so crazy with love—or just so crazy—that she really thinks she'll find her husband! And that if she finds him, he'll come home."

"I know. You know. I bet even the kids know. But Mom doesn't. Or won't admit it, I guess."

"Right. But, Casey, my point is, I feel the same way you do, but you don't see me sneaking out every night. You don't see me trying to hurt Mom."

"I come back, don't I? I may leave every night, but I always come back. Of all the times I could have left, all the boys who wanted me to run away with them, I stayed. And I'll stay this time too. Now if you'll excuse me, I've got a date."

I walk to the stairs quickly, even though I know Will won't try to stop me now. My heart is pounding, and adrenaline is coursing through my body.

This was a lot worse than most other nights. We got into a lot more than my smoking or sneaking out with boys. It's the first time we've said some of those things.

I hate to even think them.

As I'm walking to the lobby where I can see Paul standing, I light up a cigarette. He nods hello and asks whether I want to go for a ride. I say yes immediately.

He's a lot cuter than some of them, with intense blue eyes and dark brown, neatly combed hair. His build is slight, but I'm sure he works out in a gym or exercises at home, because you can tell he's really strong. He looks really clean and neat, like he probably showered for this. I appreciate that.

Twenty minutes later, we're sitting by the river in his car, one of those old Broncos that look like they could crush just about anything. We watch as a shrimp boat propels itself upstream, lights blinking in the velvety darkness. He's really fidgety, and I wonder if he's done stuff like this before. I decide to make it easy.

"So, Paul, do you want to talk?"

He looks relieved and grins, "Yeah. Sounds great."

He's adorable when he grins, because good genes and nice teeth are rare in these parts. I lean in to kiss him, but he backs away.

"What's wrong?" I'm confused. "Don't you like me?"

"Yeah. Yeah, I do."

I decide to give him a few more minutes to get used to the idea. He's a shy guy. I like that. So many others are just rude and brash, not at all worth me. He's different.

I stretch my long legs out and ask if he's got a beer. He frowns and says no, he's not into that. I shrug and light up another cigarette. He doesn't say anything, but rolls down his window all the way so I know that he's not into that either. I put it out.

"So you don't smoke, and you don't drink?"

"No. I just don't like it."

He's still watching the river. He's good-looking in profile too, though his nose may be a little larger than normal. Somehow I find that endearing. And suddenly, looking at him, I realize something else.

"You're a virgin too, aren't you?"

"Yes. And I'm going to stay that way for a while." Quiet and patient, like he's talking to a child or repeating something that he's had to say many times.

I start to resent him, and it comes out when I reply.

"So why'd you ask me here?"

"To talk. I mean, really, to talk. When you checked in with your family, you just seemed, I don't know, so miserable. I thought maybe I could help."

A bubble of anger starts in my stomach and rises up to fill my chest. Who does this guy think he is? He doesn't even know me, but he comes along making me feel bad about the way I live and then telling me that I look so miserable that he wanted to help.

Well, fuck you, Mr. Do-Gooder. What am I, this week's charity case? Poor little rich boy wants to feel better about himself, so he's got to help me out? And he expects me to appreciate this?!

He's probably got a perfect home life himself, parents still together, an adored only child, Dad works hard for the money, and Mom waits at home with dinner ready, gets A's in school, aiming for a college scholarship. What could he possibly do to help me?

"Don't do me any favors." I know there's ice in my voice. "You don't know anything about me or my family."

"I know. I ... I didn't mean to suggest that I did." He's stammering, less sure now, and I know that I've gotten the better of him. But then he looks directly at me, so earnestly that it startles and touches me in a way no other boy has. "It's just ... I thought maybe it would help to talk about it."

"Yeah, to some complete stranger. What makes you think I'd want to share that with you?" I've got to gain back the ground I lost with his look.

He's looking at me again now, in a piercing, incisive way. It makes me really uncomfortable, and so I stare fixedly out the window, closed off from his gaze and what he might sense.

"Well, you were going to sleep with me."

His answer is quiet and coolly logical, and this infuriates me. It's just the kind of thing Will would have said, the kind of thing he does say about what I do at night.

"That's different. Sex is impersonal. It's an escape, it's for fun, and if you're not into that, then I think you should just take me home. You don't know the first thing about me, and don't you ever assume that you do!"

"You're right. I don't. But can't you tell that I want to?"

What kind of bullshit story is this? What kind of person wants to get to know someone they've only talked to for a few minutes? What kind of person would even care about a life like mine, much less want in on it?

"You shouldn't. I'm a bitch. Me and my whole family. We've all got just one big fucked-up life that we share, and you shouldn't want to join. We wouldn't want to blight your happy personal world."

It's harsh, but I want to stop talking about this. It's too much on top of my fight with Will. I think my words have worked. He seems more distant, probably angry, and isn't fidgeting anymore.

"What makes you think my world is happy?"

He says it quietly, but I can tell how much emotion, especially anger, is behind it. It's a little scary, and I immediately feel bad.

"Nothing. I'm sorry. I was out of line. I don't know any more about you than you do about me. Less, in fact." I'm apologetic, but not forgiving.

We both stare out at the river again, drawn into ourselves, completely alone. The sky is light with false dawn. The real one won't be for hours yet. I look at my watch.

"I should get back."

He nods, then starts the car, and we drive back to the motel. I know better than to try a goodnight kiss. He waits until I'm inside, then drives on up the packed dirt road. I go back to the room. Will lets me in. He always waits up. Without a word I crawl into bed, feeling worse than when I left.

The next morning comes sooner than I want it to. I go through the routine of getting ready to leave. Mom is excited, because she thinks she's got a real chance of finding Dad a little further down the road, maybe back in Mississippi.

Tommy and Sarah are happy, because the desk clerk gave them lollipops. Jen looks tired, and I wonder if she stayed up with Will. Paul checks us out, and I can see Will glaring at him. I elbow Will, and he stops, reluctantly.

As he prints out our bill, Paul hands me a slip of paper. It has a number and address—his, I'm sure.

I want to throw it away, just to show him that I don't need him, like I've done with all the others, but instead, I fold it carefully and stick it in my purse. His eyes meet mine, and for a moment, it looks as though he may say something, but he closes his mouth and gives me a slight nod. I'm on my way, without a word. I feel his blue eyes following me out the door.

Maybe someday I will write him. After all, he's different.

Jen 2000

This is for all the kids out there like me.

You'll know who you are as soon as I start talking, as I pinpoint details of your life you think I couldn't possibly know about.

I do know.

I know because they're the same as mine. The same as my bed-sharing, Easy-Mac-eating, Walmart-shopping, money-owing, food-stamp-using, porch-collapsing, white-trash life. Those of you who know what I'm talking about, this is for all of you.

For anyone who's ever shared a single room in a motel with more than four people. For anyone who's had to go to school in clothes swiped from a grocery store Goodwill bin. For anyone who's ever cut school because they were too ashamed to be seen.

For anyone who's ever worn hand-me-down underwear or gone without any at all not because it's kinky, but because it's necessary. For anyone who's eaten Spam as a special treat or had a ketchup sandwich.

For anyone who's lived in a house where the vermin outnumber the kids or even the roaches think the kitchen isn't worth a visit. For anyone whose plaster walls are crumbling so much that even the pictures torn from magazines won't hide the cracks.

For anyone who dreams of being able to have plaster walls to crumble.

For all of you who have stood on dirt driveways or have really walked barefoot in the snow. For all of you who receive church charity baskets, instead of making them. For you who have been stuffed into the cabs of pickup trucks or ridden in the back, even in winter wind. For anyone whose dog looks better fed than they do.

And for all of you who've watched at windows or kept midnight vigils or just stared off into the distance at random moments in time and wondered...

Your father isn't coming back.

Your father isn't, and neither is mine.

I don't know why anyone would try to deny it. Those kids that I've bathed with, slept with, hugged, hated, comforted, and cherished, they sometimes deny it. Those siblings, all of them, seem to have a problem dealing with the obvious.

Dad's not coming back.

They all know it, but two of them are too little to admit it, one of them is gone away, probably for good, one of them likes to keep up the appearance of hope, and the other admits it so loudly and vehemently that I think she hopes, even more than the others, that she's wrong.

Let me get one thing straight before anyone gets mad at me: our family wasn't perfect before he left, either. And I know lots of families are even worse off when both parents are there. As for ours, well, I think we could have made it after he left.

We could have banded together, carried on, had a semi-normal trailer-park life. Plenty of people do, and we could have joined them if Mom hadn't flipped the hell out.

Needless to say, it's not really an option anymore. As for my father, I don't pretend that it would be good if he came back. But he wasn't like a lot of fathers. He wasn't mean to Mom, and certainly wasn't to us. He drank, but he never got mean. He just got sad. I think that's why he left.

He just got too sad.

I mean, it's one thing to watch your own life crumble. A single man can spend his days pumping gas, his nights drinking beer, and still get nothing from it, but at least the only one he's hurting is himself.

It's one thing to stand in your kitchen and realize that you're wasting your own life. It's quite another to sit in the living-room-kitchen-dining-room of a three-room house and know that while you drink their doctor bills away, your six children lie stacked in the room next door, and your wife is silently crying in the bathroom.

You may be going down, but you're taking them along for the spiraling ride, and it's a lot scarier than the Cyclone Coaster at the county fair. It's that kind of knowledge that would eat away at a man day and night. It's that kind of knowledge that could be twisted around to fit some strange logic, if you thought about it enough. It's that kind of knowledge that would drive a man to leave.

Or so I believe.

Why *would* he do it? I've asked myself the question enough times, seen it reflected in my family's faces, and heard the plaintive cries in my mind so much that by now I'd have to have a theory. This was the only thing I've come up with, since he didn't get mean, didn't get mad, didn't hurt us, didn't hurt Mom.

He just sat there quietly and hurt, period.

And if you've got enough hurt, if you hate yourself enough, you might start to think that those kids, that wife, they'd be better off without you. You might start to convince yourself that leaving would help. That your wife wouldn't cry as much with you gone, that your kids would feel better about showing their faces at school, that suddenly the house payments wouldn't be as much of a burden and there'd be more money, because you wouldn't be there to drink it up.

But you wouldn't be there to earn it either. There'd be no more money to make house payments. And your kids would have to deal with the stigma of having a father who abandoned them, instead of a poor, lazy, drunk one who is there—and, FYI, it's a lot worse to have a father who's gone. And your wife would cry more and smile less and start to go a little … funny, until finally she went funny enough that she'd take off with the five kids left to chase after what could never be.

I haven't been to school in nearly two years. I don't like it, because I know I'm smart. I don't mean to sound arrogant, but I always got A's and did as well as possible in my dead-end class filled with kids who were repeating for the second or third time.

I admit that it wasn't hard at my school, but I think even if you sent me to a ritzy prep school like Saint Agnes's, I could do really well. It's not too late. I'm only twelve. I've got plenty of time to catch up and make something of myself.

It's what Dad would want.

Of course, I can't bring this up to Mom at all, because her eyes would fill with tears at the very mention of one of us leaving. We can't leave, any of us. We can't leave ever, because after Dad and Jared, she couldn't take it. I don't blame her for having a real fear of being left, but she had to know Jared couldn't just take over like that.

Poor thing, he was only sixteen. How the hell could she have expected him to take over a job that a full-grown man ran away from? It would have scared me off too, probably faster than him.

As for Will, well, he sure is trying. He knows that, to her, he has to embody everything Dad and Jared weren't. He's got to be her perfect boy. He's got to be husband and father and brother, the Holy Trinity rolled into one tall, dark, and handsome package.

Poor, perfect Will.

I've thought about all this a lot. I understand my family better than they understand themselves. I don't sleep much. I lie awake—anonymous motel rooms, youth shelters, the back of the pickup, on the ground, it doesn't matter—I lie awake and think this through. And of course, I listen to them. It's amazing the things people say and do when they think everyone else is asleep.

Will and Jared had some pretty impressive fights before he left, but nothing beats the ones Will and Casey have now. I guess it would be a natural big-brother reaction, whether or not Dad left us, but I think Will's hypersensitive on the subject.

I'm sure it has to do with Mom. I mean, Oedipus complex aside, how could it not? Between my mom and my sister, I'll bet I know more about sex than any other twelve-year-old girl out there. I don't just mean what it is or how it's done, but what it can get you. The obvious answer is money, and that's what Will keeps telling himself—and Casey—that Mom is in it for. My own opinion is that money's certainly a nice fringe benefit. But I think Mom is more like Casey than Will wants to admit. She likes the escape and attention just as much. And for her it's far less risky, since she has her tubes tied.

I'm kind of shocked that Casey isn't pregnant yet, since I know for a fact she doesn't have birth control pills—like she could even get them at age sixteen in this backwater county. She's probably smart enough to make them use condoms. I caught her buying some once from a machine in a gas station bathroom. She wasn't embarrassed at all. In fact, I'm surprised she didn't offer me one.

She'd probably fuck whoever in full view of all of us, if only to spite Will and force Mom to wake the hell up. At least she's smart enough to watch out for herself that way. There's nothing worse she could do than add another kid to this family.

I'm not sure why Will's so squeamish about it. I know he's not a virgin. He's damn good looking, and girls have been throwing themselves at him for years. When I was six and he was twelve, he made me sit on a stump in the driveway and watch the house for him while he and Rosetta Thompson got busy in the bush behind me.

He was twelve! That's my age! So why he has such a problem with Casey at sixteen I can't really say.

Anyway, he won't have to worry about me. I'm not going to start having sex anytime soon. It's not because of any puritanical values or some grand moral commitment. It's not even for my sake so much as for the boys. If I'm anything like my mother or sister, in fact, it's downright dangerous for those boys.

I'm pretty. I know it. I won't pretend about that either. You can hate me for admitting right out that I'm both pretty and smart, but before you do, keep in mind that I also admit we're dirt poor, fucked up, and that my father isn't coming back.

Anyway, I'm pretty. Casey is pretty too, although she messes it up with makeup and piercings and all that kind of stuff. My mother is very pretty, even though the nicotine-stained teeth and fingers sort of take away from it. I'm never going to smoke either, because I've spent way too much time in the car being nauseated by the smell of cigarettes.

The point is, we're all pretty. We could all get boys as easily as you please. Even I can. I'm just twelve, but I'm fairly well developed already. But wherever they go, Casey and Mom I mean, they leave behind heartbroken men.

It's usually the other way around where one night stands are concerned, but something about the women in my family cries out for attention and soothing and a male presence … at least that's what the men seem to think. What they really cry out for is escape. They don't need those men the way the men want to be needed.

All men want to be needed, but not too much. It's a delicate balance, and it's one Casey and Mom flatly refuse to give them. They use them for sex, and they use sex for distraction. When they're done being distracted, they leave the men behind. Just like that. Jilted girls everywhere can have a private giggle at the expense of these guys.

Mom won't be satisfied with any man besides Dad, and Casey won't be satisfied with any man. Mom makes money and feels for a while that her life is worth something. Casey has some fun, forgetting that the next bed she'll sleep in will be with me and Sarah.

I know Casey's been the first time for a lot of boys and that it would kill them to know that they're just another face in the crowd to her. They think of her all the time.

I've almost never seen her come home without a slip of paper in her hand, another name and number. She throws them out. Sometimes, if she's feeling particularly nasty, she'll throw them out in front of the boy, maybe even hand it right back as though to say, "Don't lie to yourself, pal."

I hear them outside, telling her how much she means to them and hear her casually brush them off:

"Casey, I barely even know you, but I think I love you."

"Hey, can I have one of your cigarettes?"

They can't have her, and they know it. And she knows that they know it. And she's the only one who could possibly change that for them. It's a tremendous amount of power to have. It's really the only thing she can have power over, so of course she loves it.

Will hates not being able to control her. I think he knows that he's really just filling in. He's not a parent, not even the oldest son. He knows he doesn't have power or the right to it. He tries, tries really hard, to become the person Mom needs him to be, but of course he can't be that. No one could.

Not even Dad, and that's why he left.

Sometimes I wonder if Will might leave too. I know he must consider it every once in a while. He waits up for Casey every time she leaves. I don't think he knows that I'm almost always awake and almost always watching. He waits, gazing out into the night, lighting the occasional cigarette. In that regard, he's no angel, though he wouldn't want anyone to guess it.

I know for a fact that I am the only person in the family who knows about his cigarettes. I haven't said anything because with the way he yells at Casey, it would make him seem like a huge hypocrite. I don't want to deal his self-esteem yet another blow.

This is what he's doing now: staring into the night while a cigarette smolders. He's sitting outside in the moonlight. He's a damn fool for not staying in. For once we have an air conditioner in this motel room, and it is a Louisiana summer. Is he trying to be some sort of martyr by sitting in the humidity?

All it's really going to do is make his clothes smell tomorrow and deprive him of what little time he could spend in the cool. You couldn't pay me to get out of this bed and sit outside. But if he wants to that's his choice.

"Jen?"

It's Sarah's thick, sleepy voice. Between me and Casey the poor kid never gets a good night's sleep.

"Yeah, Sar?"

"Is it morning?"

"No. It's too dark to be morning, see?"

"Did Casey leave again?"

"Yes."

"Mama said not to."

She turns accusing brown eyes on me, as though I'm the one who didn't listen. Sometimes I think she mixes up me and Casey or just assumes we're all the same. Such a cynic by age seven, I hate to think what she'll be like by the time she gets to be as old as me.

"I know."

"I *told* her Mama said not to... ."

"I heard you. You're a good girl, Sarah."

She gives a weak smile and fingers her rust-colored hair, snarled by lying on the pillow.

"Will you braid my hair tomorrow?"

"Sure."

"Two pigtails?"

"Three, if you like."

That gets her. She giggles softly and turns over in bed so that she's curled up against me. Why kids always want to cuddle when it is so hot, I'll never know. I never used to. But since I know she likes it, I wrap my arms around her. Let her find comfort where she can. Soon she's asleep by my side.

The door clicks open, and Will comes back inside. His dark hair is plastered to his forehead with sweat, and he almost steams in the sudden blast of cold. He closes the door soundlessly and pads into the bathroom. He comes out clutching Casey's plaid shirt scrunched into a little ball. It used to be Jared's. He sits on the floor in front of the window unit, leaning against her side of the bed, pressing his face into the material and crying.

He doesn't make any noise, but I know he's crying anyway. He does it every once in a while. I've never asked what makes him do it, and I don't need to. People who don't know him would say it must be for Dad, but they weren't close enough for that. Will only let one person touch him, only allowed one person to truly know him, and that person was Jared.

He's crying for Jared. They were only ten months apart, in the same class at school; everyone thought they were twins. They might as well have been a lot of the time. They had a language all their own, one that didn't even need words.

That's why I think Will knew Jared was planning to leave. It shocked the rest of us, especially since Jared was always so quiet and cautious, but Will had to have known. Will and Jared could tell everything about each other, right down to who would want an extra apple at school or when the other needed corroboration on a lie. There is just no way Jared hid something like this from Will. So Will knew.

But for how long?

And why didn't he stop him? Was it a choice between Jared and Will? One of us stays, and one of us goes, so *Here, bro, I'll flip you for it.* Only one of us gets to have a life. And if that's the case, did Will win or lose?

I shift slightly in the bed to let him know that I'm at least somewhat awake. He stops crying abruptly, shuddering slightly as he does so. He spreads the shirt out over his knees and folds it gently. He rubs his hands over his face and breathes deeply. He stares off into space, and I wish that I could ask him what's wrong, but I already know it's useless. He'd try to protect me, a nice idea, but totally impractical. The best we can ever hope to do is comfort each other, but for tonight, even this is out.

I hear footsteps on the creaky wooden steps of the motel. Casey makes a lot less noise leaving than coming back. I think she wants to make sure there's someone there to let her in. She doesn't have to worry. There always will be.

Will knows his role and opens the door as she reaches it.

They stare at each other for a moment, an identical challenge in each stubborn face. At the same time, they both seem to decide the tough exterior isn't worth the effort. They relax, both looking drained, exhausted. Casey shivers as the sweat that covers her body in a thin film meets the full blast of the air conditioner. Will unfolds the shirt and drapes it around her shoulders, leaving his arm there a bit longer in a small hug.

"Goodnight, Casey," he says as he heads back to his sleeping bag at the foot of Mom's bed.

She doesn't say anything back, just slides in next to me, trying her best not to disturb us too much.

If only she knew.

David 2001/1977

My first acid trip was a bad one.

I don't remember much about it except for that. It was a Technicolor nightmare of bugs and corpses and Lyndon Johnson, all echoing to the tune of *Hey, hey, LBJ, how many kids did you kill today*? The world that I thought was real was melting around me and giving way to a circus of maniacal, cannibalistic clowns and a ringmaster who wanted nothing more than to mount my head atop the tent.

I'm told that I spent the entire time screaming for help, and when I woke up everyone was positive that I'd been to hell and back. It sure felt that way. Those poor, burned-out heads of the Seventies, only some of whom had been to the jungle and had real reasons to scream, looked at me with glazed eyes and offered me a joint in consolation.

"Sorry, man. I can't believe your first one was a bust. I promise, next time will be like heaven."

I never found out about any next time, because my first time scared the shit out of me. I hoped never to have that feeling again in my life. But I haven't been so lucky.

The past five years have been like a bad acid trip that I can't seem to wake up from. I guess I'm having trouble accepting that it's just life now.

I left the drugs—at least all the hardcore ones—behind, once I met Amy. Still, she was never the most straight-edged girl herself. In fact, the way I met her isn't a fit story to tell my children, not that that's a problem now.

It was the summer of 1976, in a quiet Alabama town. The war was over, and we won. Or, rather, that's what they—the ever-present *they*, familiar to anyone who grew up in the Seventies—would have us believe. We knew, of course, that we had lost. The way those boys were coming home, how could we help knowing?

I was eighteen and sighing with relief that I'd never have to go off the way I'd seen my brother Brian do. I'd also never have to come home in a box like Brian either. Or maybe, instead, lie in some anonymous military cemetery where all the graves look alike.

I had an older sister who dragged me along to protest marches and die-ins from the time I was twelve until she didn't need to drag me anymore. I grew up with her on the frontlines of the unacceptable and disgraceful, and I know our parents paid for that.

But they let us do as we liked, do as they couldn't bear to do, because we'd all made our sacrifice. They paid with a son, we paid with a brother, and we felt for the families like ours. Our parents understood those looks from neighbors and the usual question whispered to them over glasses of iced tea: "Don't you think it's time you did something about those kids?"

But our parents always deflected the question by saying something bland and inoffensive, like "We think they are old enough to make their own choices."

And we chose. We chose to ride together with black people on Freedom buses, and we chose to get high sharing joints with people we didn't know and would never see again. We chose to be different from our neighbors and even most of our friends.

We were David and Charisma—my sister had chosen that name because Margaret didn't seem to suit her anymore. We were bit players in the movement to stop the war, end racism, guarantee a woman's right to choose, and get equal pay for equal work.

Hard to believe now, but I marched in those kinds of marches. I liked to think of myself as progressive. Besides, I have to admit, it was a great way to meet girls who were, in the jargon of the time, *in command of their own sexuality*, and so were likely to act on their impulses without much persuasion. I spent my teenage years fighting for one cause or another, feeling pretty damned good that I could do it all here in the good old U.S. of A. and wouldn't have to join the military and fight a foreign enemy in some faraway country.

2

It was during the summer of '76, when I was about to graduate from high school, that I started hanging around with Joe Conway.

Every small town has someone like Joe Conway. To the parents of Melville, where I grew up, he was the devil in size-eleven shoes. He drank beer and smoked cigarettes, and sometimes, as the proper southern women would say, he smoked *other things* as well.

The parents in my town despised Joe Conway, and Joe, in turn, despised them right back. In fact, he pretty much despised everyone, even those few people he let hang around with him. That was the summer before I was supposed to head off to college at Louisiana State University in Baton Rouge, and I was so impatient and bored that I yearned to experience something as far removed from the day-to-day tedium of Melville as I could get.

Joe was what I could get.

As long as I supplied the beer for his weekly parties, I could get in and avail myself of whatever was being offered for free. This was no small privilege, because Joe was Melville's answer to Hugh Hefner, as well as a big-time dealer. His apartment, above a pawn shop run by his older brother, was out on the state highway, far away from any other residence. His all-night parties couldn't bother the neighbors, because there weren't any.

It was at one of Joe's parties that I had my bad acid trip—and nearly scared to death the girl I was attempting to seduce at the time. About three parties after that, I came in, already buzzed, and noticed a girl I'd never seen before blowing smoke rings into Eddie Castello's face.

Eddie was laughing as though it was the funniest, cutest thing ever, but you could see that he was annoyed and only putting up with it because of the hopes he entertained about the girl's slim body that was barely concealed by her thin cotton dress. She was just as obviously bored with Eddie and not planning on allowing him to realize his hopes at any point in the night.

Any new girl, especially one as attractive as her, was rare at these parties. I decided I'd save Eddie from additional humiliation, so I filled a paper cup with the cheap beer I had brought and made my way over to where she was standing.

"Nectar of the gods," I said. I offered her the cup.

"And I thought it was cat piss," she said. She took the cup and gave me a guarded smile.

Eddie said nothing to either of us, just turned and walked over to the table where the beer coolers were.

"I'll only drink this because I watched you pour it and know that you didn't put something in it."

"Now why would I do that?"

"Well, that's a silly question."

She raised the cup to her lips and downed the beer in one long gulp. She handed the cup back to me, piercing me with her steady blue eyes. Then, unexpectedly, she reached behind her back and unzipped her dress. It fell to the floor, and she stood there, completely naked.

I felt my face flush, and if other people turned to look, I didn't notice. My eyes were fixed on her.

"What's the matter?" She gave a little laugh and looked straight at me. "I'm not shy, so why should you be? Joe paid me for a show, but maybe you aren't...up...for it."

Her smile became mischievous. She spoke patiently, as if explaining something to a child, but her smile and silky tone implied that she knew that I only used to be a child.

Joe or somebody put on a record of Abba's *Dancing Queen*, and the eyes of all the dozen or so people in the room were fixed on her as she moved her body to the music.

She gave Joe his money's worth. That's why I could never tell my kids about how I met their mother.

3

Amy was sixteen and destitute.

She had been kicked out of her parents' house. She was from two towns over, Pike's Creek, and her parents had finally had enough of her antics. She didn't turn what happened into a sob story, just explained it one day as she helped me pick up the beer from the Bon-Ton Market.

This was one of the things that I liked most about her. Her life may have been hard, but that didn't mean she was weak. She knew she wasn't, and she wanted everyone else to know it as well.

"No great loss," she said over her shoulder, stretching to the top shelf for another six-pack, her plaid skirt rising to just below her buttocks. "My father shouldn't have had a problem with me, anyway. He was probably just mad that I wouldn't put out for him."

This shocked what I thought of as my free-thinking mind.

"You, you mean he... ."

"Nah." She shook her head. "I think he wanted it a couple of times, because he's just a man. And my mom is a frigid, pious bitch." Her tone was matter-of-fact, and she gave a dismissive shrug. "Hey, let's get some peanuts this time too."

Amy became a regular at Joe's parties, and I was her partner-in-crime. The other boys complained about it for a while, but she would refuse to do anything if it wasn't with someone she liked. And I, for whatever reason, was someone she liked.

As that long, sticky summer drew to a close, I began to realize that very soon I would be leaving town, something I was glad about. But I would also be leaving Amy, and I wasn't glad about that.

I brought this up to her one day, as we lay stretched out on the white sheets of a double bed in the spare room of Joe's empty apartment. With the blinds pulled and the lights off, we were trying to find some relief from the heat of the late summer.

"I'm not staying, you know," I said, not looking at her.

"I know," she said. "Men never do. And if they do stay it's usually when they shouldn't."

"But doesn't it *bother* you?"

"That you're going?"

"Yeah."

I raised myself up on one elbow. She was still lying on her back, feet tangled in the sheets, the rest of her body exposed. Her feet always got cold, even in the hottest weather. Not looking at me, she frowned at the ceiling.

"Did you know there's a crack right by the light bulb that looks like a dog's head?"

"Amy?"

"What?" She continued staring at the ceiling. Then, with a reluctant sigh, she said, "Oh, you really want me to answer."

"Well, yeah."

"Even if you won't like it?" She sounded sad.

"Yeah, might as well." I spoke quickly, thinking I might change the response she was hinting at. "But you should know that ... ."

She gave me a sharp look, her eyes blue blanks and empty.

"David, please don't tell me you're in love with me." Her voice had a hard edge.

That stopped me dead, because I had been about to say just that. It was true too. Despite the way we'd met and the things we'd done, what I looked forward to wasn't the exhibitionistic shows at Joe's Saturday parties, but the days in between them when we would buy Cokes at the filling station and sit in the car and talk, or go for hamburgers at the Dairy Queen, or just wander around downtown window shopping. Now I was nearly struck dumb.

"But why not?"

"Oh, that is what you were going to say, wasn't it? Why do men always think they love me? They don't, really." She gave a wry smile. "They just confuse it with wanting to fuck me."

I opened my mouth to speak, but she cut me off.

"I suppose you're going to tell me that you're different."

I had been about to say exactly that.

"I am." I said it anyway. "I would want to be with you, even if no sex was involved. I don't want to leave you. I want to stay and find out more about you ... *everything* about you. Amy, I do love you."

She paused, and when she spoke the harshness in her voice was gone. She took my hand, sitting up now to look into my eyes, and she spoke earnestly to me, as she had only a few times before.

"But you got into college. You'd better go, or you'll never leave this town. David, you deserve better."

"Then come with me."

"I can't go to college. And I'm sixteen, remember?"

"I meant come to LSU with me. You can live with me, and I'll find you another job and ... ."

"What's wrong with the job I've got?"

Not defensive or offended, she meant it as a real question. I had trouble treating it that way, because the answer was so glaringly obvious to me.

"Well, it's ... I mean ... if you were living with me, you couldn't keep doing it."

"Why not? It's *my* life." She gave me an earnest look. "Making you a part of it doesn't mean I should have to change everything to suit you."

"But you could do better."

"Better? What's better?" Her voice rose to a higher pitch. "Punching cash register keys at the drugstore? Serving greasy burgers to pimply kids who think a dime is a good-sized tip? Long hours, low pay? And most of all, David, no fun."

I started to interrupt her, but I caught myself.

"What I do now pays well and is always in demand." She gave me one of her mischievous smiles. "And as you of all people *should* have noticed, it's something I enjoy."

She paused a moment, as if deciding what she was going to say next. I felt the tension of the moment and didn't speak.

"I'll come with you," Amy said at last. "But I won't give up my life for you." She cocked her head and looked at me. "Do we agree?"

We did, I did.

4

When I left for LSU that August, Amy came along.

I rode with my parents in our Ford Country Squire station wagon with my suitcases, books, and records. Amy took the bus. I gave her money for the fare, and she didn't hold it against me for my not wanting my parents to know that we were going off together.

We met up again at the ramshackle three-story white frame house that was owned by the university. Freshmen weren't guaranteed a room in the dorms, so off-campus housing was the solution to the overcrowding.

This turned out to be good luck for me, because I could never have kept Amy's presence hidden from the authorities in an on-campus dormitory. Instead of a single room shared with another freshman, I was assigned to a suite with two bedrooms, a small living room, and a shared bathroom. The two lower floors had the same configuration, and each floor had a kitchenette in the hall. The house was only a block from the campus and on a street lined with tall oak trees hung with long tendrils of Spanish moss. Overall, it wasn't a bad place to live.

After meeting my roommate, Roger Morris, the first thing I told him was that my girlfriend was going to be living with us. Despite the thick lenses of his black-framed Buddy Holly glasses, I could see his eyes open wide in surprise. But almost instantly, he smiled, and I thought I could detect a look of delighted anticipation.

"Great," he said. "The more the merrier."

I considered taking Roger aside and making it clear to him that Amy was mine and that's why she was living with me. He was there just because we were, well, assigned to be roommates.

I was on the verge of delivering this speech, when I glanced at Amy and realized that it would be a big mistake.

"I'm Amy," she said, shaking hands with Roger.

She gave him a broad smile. I came to recognize that smile, the longer I knew her, as her favorite from her repertoire of come-hither looks. The smile managed to suggest that since the three of us were going to be living together anyway, why not have a little extra fun? If Roger had been inclined to object to Amy staying with us, he gave no sign of it. I wasn't as pleased with the smile as Roger seemed to be, but I said nothing.

Roger was a clean-cut guy for 1976. His hair was barely longer than his collarbone, and his sideburns wouldn't have been noticed at a Republican convention. He had terrible eyesight, and his face was defined by those black frames with their Coke-bottle lenses. He hadn't had a girlfriend in high school, so having Amy around was a novel experience for him.

As many probably had before him, Roger lost his virginity during a beer-fueled, late-night passionate encounter with Amy. I was technically present, but I was in my room asleep or passed out, hard to say which. The practical result was that if there had ever been a chance that Roger was going to complain to the university authorities about Amy living with us, it evaporated like snow in August.

Sometimes, I think Amy is right and that men are more easily manipulated than toddlers asking for ice cream. We want just one thing, and if you give it to us, we'll stay as loyal as a lap dog. That was true of Roger and virtually all the men I had seen swarm around Amy, even when she had all her clothes on.

But I was very much aware of Amy's bag of tricks and wasn't particularly susceptible to any of them. Maybe this was because I had had a lot of experience with girls, grown women, and people in general during all those marches, sit-ins, and freedom rides that Maggie and I had participated in before Amy even showed up on my radar. Or maybe I was just different from the other men she had met and charmed with nothing more than a smile. Maybe that's why she was attracted to me enough to follow me to Baton Rouge. That's what I like to believe, but how true it is I don't know.

5

During that year, Amy and I never settled into anything as formal as a routine. Even so, we often shopped for groceries and usually fixed dinner in the kitchenette that we shared with two other students on the third floor of what the university grandly called the DeBakey House. Roger took his meals in the university cafeteria, so we usually ate by ourselves in the sitting room of our suite.

Other than eating most of our meals together, the rest of the time we both came and went more or less as we pleased. I went to classes without her, of course, but I also sometimes went to parties by myself. She went out on her own, sometimes all night, and I never asked her where she had been. She also never volunteered that information.

She was living her life as she wanted, and although I was a part of it, she never treated me as if I were someone from whom she needed to get permission before doing something. I accepted that, even though I sometimes wanted to tell her what I thought she should do, just for her own benefit.

To be honest, aside from the pleasure of seeing her, the best thing about her coming home was that she usually returned with a wad of cash. I never asked her if she stole it or if she was paid for doing something, because I didn't want to know.

I never tried to make her stop either, not up until the day that ended everything.

6

We had a terrific fight right before my spring finals.

It was a blisteringly hot day with stifling humidity, and that made our fight all the worse. I thought for sure that she was going to walk out of my life forever, and that I'd spend the rest of my days chasing her.

Fate really has an ironic side sometimes.

The heat was unseasonable for late April, and of course our ramshackle excuse for a dorm had no air conditioning. I had plugged in an oscillating fan I had brought from home, but it did little more than move the hot air in lazy circles through the room, like convection currents in an oven.

Roger and I sat at opposite ends of our tiny third-floor sitting room. We were each wearing nothing but boxer shorts, in an attempt to get as cool as possible. Both of us had books open on our laps. Roger was studying for his chemistry final, and I was doing my best to understand Mill's *On Liberty*. I had discovered that I had a real affinity for philosophy, and I wanted to ace my exam.

We were both concentrating as much as the heat would allow. Now and then Roger would clean the fog off his glasses, and I would wipe the sweat off my forehead with my sodden handkerchief. The only sounds in the room were the turning of pages and the low buzzing of the fan.

Then Amy breezed in, looking marvelously unaffected by the weather. She'd climbed in through Mark Hampton's first-floor window, like always, and probably spending a little time with Mark on the way.

Roger jumped up and swore, more at himself than at her, and hurriedly began pulling on a pair of trousers. I regarded him with amusement. No matter how many times Amy had seen him without anything on at all, he insisted on maintaining what he considered appropriate behavior when she was around, and that included wearing pants.

She took no notice of him, except to give him a slightly sardonic smile. Instead, she sat herself in my lap, right on top of the book I had been reading, in the same way that cats do when they want to ensure your full attention. She ran her fingers through my damp hair so that it stood up in spikes, then kissed me full on the mouth before speaking.

"Hey, you want to go out with me tonight?"

That may not sound unusual, but for Amy it most certainly was. Very early in our relationship, she had given me to understand that I was not her only man, though I was one she favored above others, and that I shouldn't press her on anything, or she'd be gone for good.

Along with that, I was silently instructed not to ask her where she was going, who she was with, or whether I could go too. In return, she would favor me with a special status and the occasional hit of pot when I wanted it, as well as sex, which the other boys also got.

In the beginning this had been rocky. I wanted her to be my girlfriend in a conventional way, and that just wasn't on her agenda. She dictated the terms, and as soon as I became reasonably comfortable with that, we got on well.

I'd be lying if I said that lately the arrangement had gotten to me more than it used to. It hadn't. That's part of what made our fight so terrible. It wasn't the culmination of any build-up or anything like that. It was just so damn strange. We'd been going along just fine, no surprises, when all of a sudden, she asks if I want to go out with her.

I guess that's how I knew something was up.

"Can't," I said, smiling. "I've got my philosophy final tomorrow at nine. Maybe if it was statistics, I could get blitzed tonight and do okay, but you've got to be able to think for a philosophy exam." I shrugged. "I'm sorry."

She didn't look annoyed yet.

She probably figured she could get me in a few easy moves. She didn't say anything, but she shifted around on my lap so that she was straddling me. She looked straight into my eyes and began to slide her hand under my boxer shorts and up my thigh. I took hold of her wrist and stopped her, even as I felt myself begin to respond.

"Amy, I really can't. I'm sorry."

"You sure?"

I turned loose of her wrist, and leaning to the side, she reached into her pocket and pulled out a small plastic bag of white powder. She let me glimpse it, then immediately shoved it back into her pocket.

She didn't want to trigger a rant from Roger. We weren't addicts; we smoked pot occasionally and snorted coke rarely. We stayed away from heroin, and I never wanted to risk anything like my first terrible acid trip. But Roger disapproved of all drugs, and we tried to avoid testing his patience.

Most times I would have yielded to temptation, but not this time. I really wanted to do as well on that final as I had been doing in the class. It was the one class that I had never skipped, and the only one I was pulling an A in.

Lowering my voice to keep from interrupting Roger, I said, "It looks like a lot of fun, but why do you need me now? You never have before."

I knew immediately that I'd hit a sore spot.

Amy swung herself off my lap, and not looking at me, she got a pack of Marlboros out of her purse. She lit one with a butane lighter, making the stifling air of the room even more unbearable. I wished Roger would say something, but he was pretending to be completely engrossed in studying.

"Would you put that out?" I said. "It's already hard to breathe in here."

Amy turned toward me, then leaning over, blew a puff of smoke in my face. I felt an urge to hit her or shove her, but I wasn't raised to hurt people, particularly not women. No matter how drunk I got, that was just something I would never do.

I stood up and snatched the cigarette out of her hand, then bent over and stubbed it out on the scarred green linoleum floor.

"You want to take care of my health too?" Amy's face was red with rage. "Maybe you ought to be more worried about that when you fuck me, David!" She was yelling now. "And why not run my whole life, like the middle-class, middle-American intellectual you want to be?"

She had hit on the real reason I didn't want to go out, and she got it on the first try. Amy possessed some special power or she wouldn't have been able to pull something like that out of the air, something I hadn't even fully admitted to myself.

Because I did want something better, I didn't want to waste my time with Amy and her friends.

I loved studying philosophy. I loved learning to ask questions that were so basic that I had never thought of them before and struggled to imagine how they could be answered. Most of all, I loved learning how to think—how to frame arguments, follow complex lines of reasoning, and, if possible, discover the weak spots.

The truth was that the life Amy and I shared was a sad and sorry substitute for the life we could be living.

I wanted to give up the drugs and the booze. I wanted to get clean, and get her clean and settle down in a nice house in some nice town. I wanted to teach high-school students or university kids to stop them from being what I had been and get them to see the truth and the light, the *veritas et lux*, that the smug Ivy Leaguers yapped about on TV.

I wanted the suit and tie, the faux leather briefcase crammed with books and papers, the meatloaf and mashed potatoes, and the two-point-five kids welcoming me home from the office. I didn't want racism or authoritarianism, but otherwise, I now wanted the life I had rebelled against since before puberty.

I hadn't admitted any of that to myself, and I wouldn't do so fully until many years later, when some of it had been achieved—the two-point-five kids at least. At that moment, I just thought I wanted to stay in and study for my final. But the truth of what Amy said explains why I jumped on her like I did.

"Intellectual?" I turned toward her. "What do you mean by that? Is wanting grades good enough to keep the scholarship I worked my ass off for being a goddamn intellectual?"

Amy's face was expressionless.

"Does wanting to keep my wits about me enough to try something that's not crack or pot, something like *philosophy*, make me a fag *intellectual*?"

I was on automatic, the words pouring out without my thinking about what I was saying.

"This isn't fucking Harvard ... it's not even fucking *Michigan* ... this is Louisiana, baby. And if I want to get far away from where I started, I have to work harder than I ever imagined I could. I don't want to blow what's probably the only chance I've got."

Then my tone became nasty. "So why don't you take yourself and your bag of cocaine and go get high with the rest of your gonna-be-nothing-forever friends while I try to *study. Okay?*"

Roger had closed his book somewhere during my outburst and grabbed the T-shirt beside his chair. By the time I had finished, he had wriggled into the shirt and headed for the door into the hall. He was evidently trying to escape before all hell broke loose.

A sense of hopelessness swept over me, and I felt the urge to follow Roger out the door. I wanted to not be in the room, not to have to deal with the consequences of everything I had just said.

She had let her purse fall to the ground and was staring at me, her face a frozen mask. She was like a boxer who knows he can drop his opponent with a single blow, but is ready to toy with him for the amusement of the crowd.

Looking at her cool anger, I suddenly became aware that I was wearing nothing but boxer shorts and that with my hair in sweaty spikes and my still grasping the limp paperback copy of Mill, I probably didn't cut an imposing figure.

I threw the book against the wall, then began pulling on my khaki pants. I wanted to give Amy the impression that I was still in charge of myself and wasn't as vulnerable as she had already perceived me to be.

"Well, aren't you high and mighty?" Amy's voice was smooth and icy, like a gin and tonic. "I had no idea you were so goddamn brilliant. I should have called you a savant, instead of an intellectual." She gave me a sardonic smile. "I fuck smart people as well as dumb ones, so I pick up a few words."

I turned away from her and finished zipping up my khakis.

"Maybe you should be a professor here, instead of a student, you're so smart. Maybe I should just call you that."

She spoke slowly and without overt anger. The voice was not Amy's at all. That, more than anything she said, gave me the chills.

"Professor, honey, you think my friends and me are going to stay shit forever? So what makes you different? Didn't we *meet* because we had the same friends? And now you stand there, dripping sweat in your J.C. Penney pants and tell me that *I'm* going to be nothing?"

I didn't meet her eyes.

"I pull in more money in a day than you could in a month from whatever chickenshit job you could get. If I wanted a mink coat, I could get it from some nice rich gentleman eager to please a seventeen-year-old, white-trash honey who ran away from an abusive father. And half the time, I wouldn't have to do anything but smile."

I turned to see her displaying the fake smile that I was familiar with from watching her charm strangers at parties.

"The other half of the time, I can make good money and get little treats like that baggie in my purse. And you know what, Professor Davy, I *like* the life I'm living. So don't you dare try to change me."

I was on the verge of objecting, but she saw the indignant look on my face and continued her rant before I could say anything.

"Oh, I know that's not what you've got in mind, at least not right now. But in the long run—and I know you want us to have a long run, Davy—you're going to want to turn me into somebody else's idea of respectable."

I said nothing.

"You don't fool me for a minute." She gave another smile that was more of a smirk. "You've been to parties less and less, and I know you've been clean from drugs for at least a month!"

She was right, and I had been avoiding drugs. I told myself that it was to keep up my grades, save my scholarship, and so save my ass. But maybe the real reason was that drugs didn't fit into my only dimly acknowledged long-term plan. Successful middle-class men could be drinkers, but not druggies. That was one of the lessons I'd absorbed during my time on marches with my sister.

"Is that why you came here?" I asked, hoping to divert Amy from further speculating about my aspirations. "To test me and see if I was going to stay clean?"

"I came here to tell you I'm pregnant," she said.

Her gaze was steady and unblinking, and although her voice was soft, it evoked in me a threat of danger that I had never felt before.

7

Either I consciously decided to sit down or my knees simply gave way. In any case, I found myself sitting on the chair where I had been reading and staring at the door to the hall.

Amy paced back and forth across the green linoleum floor in front of me. She was still talking, but I wasn't taking in anything she was saying. I seemed to have developed a form of deafness, and I seemed unable to take in the reality of her pregnancy.

That Amy might get pregnant was something that had crossed my mind. How could it not? So many times with so many men. I had been scared before, only to have my fears laid to rest by the contents of the bathroom trash can.

But of course the unexpected happens. That's why we have a word for it.

"Amy, you need to quit now," I said.

I can't clearly recall before or after I said this. It doesn't really matter, because it was the words that got her attention.

She stopped pacing and turned toward me. I thought she was about to start screaming at me again about how no one should ever try to change her, but instead, she collapsed to the floor beside my chair and started crying.

I had no idea about what to do and sat frozen. I understood plenty about sex, thanks to Amy and the liberated girls I met during sit-ins and peace marches. But when it came to dealing with a real emotional crisis, I was as clueless as a fifteen-year-old boy fumbling with his first bra strap.

And considering all the many experiences that Amy and I had shared during our time together, crying was not on the list. Without thinking about it, I had assumed that Amy was invincible, but without intending to and without even realizing what was happening, I was the one who broke her down.

And was I responsible? Was I the father?

Maybe I was callous in the face of her distress, but that's the question that kept running through my head. Had she come to me because she knew that it was me? Or had she come to me because she knew that I would be the one who would take care of her?

Even if the baby wasn't mine, I would take care of her. I really did love her, and you don't throw out the people you love. At that moment, I was filled with the desire to prove to her that I loved her and that it wasn't just her body that I cared about.

"We can get married, if that's what you want," I said. I put my hand on her head and stroked her hair. "Even if the baby isn't mine, I'm good with that. We can raise it together."

Without thinking about it, I was offering not only to help her, but to lay the foundation for the middle-class life I saw in the future for her and me.

It was exactly the wrong thing to say.

She raised her face from my lap where she'd buried it, shook off my hand and looked up at me. I had been stroking her hair as if she were a child, then it occurred to me that, at seventeen, she really was.

She seemed too exhausted from her emotional outburst to be truly angry, but I could sense the same flame burning in her as before.

"You don't think I'm *keeping* it, do you?"

I was stunned, because the possibility of abortion had never occurred to me. True, we were halfway into 1977, and a woman's right to choose had been on the books for nearly five years. True, I had marched with Maggie—or Charisma—in many demonstrations in favor of reproductive rights. True, I supported wholeheartedly a woman's right to choose. But I never thought of those anonymous would-be babies as mine. I never thought that one of those righteous unwed moms might be my fiery girlfriend.

I was struck dumb again and couldn't come up with a fast answer to her question. That was okay, because she didn't seem to expect one. She got up from the floor, walked into my room, and curled up on my bed. Despite the heat and humidity, she drew the sheet around her.

She began to cry quietly, and for the next hour or so, I sat beside her, rubbing her back. I had never heard her cry before, but now it seemed that she would never stop.

8

Through the open door, I saw Roger poke his head in, then withdraw it almost immediately. I had seen him looking at the spiral notebook that he had left open by his chair.

I got up from the bed, leaving Amy, exhausted by crying, on the verge of sleep. I picked up the notebook and opened the door to the suite and caught Roger before he had gone downstairs.

"Here, Roger."

I waved the notebook at him. He was halfway down the stairs, but when he saw me, he came back up.

"What's wrong?" he asked, taking the notebook from me. Behind his glasses, his eyes were wide and full with what I realized was genuine concern.

I ran a hand through my hair and blew out a breath I wasn't even aware that I'd been holding.

"Amy is pregnant," I said.

I figured that as my roommate he deserved some explanation of the explosive scene that had ruined his studying and made him hurry out of the room. Plus, he knew Amy, so I knew he would care about her. And to be honest, I think I also wanted someone to talk to about it.

"Oh, God." Roger's eyes grew even wider, and his face took on a deer-in-the-headlights look. "Does she know whose it is?"

This, of course, meant *Is it mine*?

Roger, like any man, wanted to know if he was suddenly going to be faced with a situation that would fundamentally alter the rest of his life. But, not to sell him short, he was a hell of a lot more concerned than most guys would have been. I think he really cared for her.

"She ... ." I was about to say she thought it was me, just to ease his barely concealed panic. Then I considered how Amy might react if Roger quoted me. So I said, "She isn't sure."

"Jesus," he said softly. He looked down at the floor, then rubbed the toe of a scuffed sneaker on the green linoleum, making a squeaking sound.

"I know."

I resisted the urge to tell him what bothered me was that she wasn't going to keep it. I would never be able to guess who the father was by noticing that the baby had Roger's lousy vision or David's nose or Mark's green eyes. That bothered me a hell of a lot more than the doubtful paternity.

But I didn't say any of it.

"When we were ... together, I wanted to use one, but she said it was okay." He looked like a little boy, in sneakers and a plain white T-shirt, his khakis wrinkled by the heat. "I thought she was on the pill. Wasn't she, David?"

"I guess. I know she couldn't have been that careless."

"Then how ...?"

He didn't finish the question. His thick hair flopped over his bewildered face and, if not for his afternoon stubble, I could have believed he was twelve again.

"How should I know?" I suddenly felt angry. "Maybe she was too hung over to take the damn thing every day! She might have missed a couple of days and figured it wouldn't matter, when *anyone* with half a brain knows that you have to take the goddamn pill every fucking day."

I broke off at the look on Roger's face. He plainly had not known that.

"Look, Roger, I'm sorry," I said, sighing. "I'm trying to make sense out of all this, and with of all things, my philosophy final tomorrow." I gave a bitter laugh. "Does intention make an act good or bad or is it the consequences of the act?"

I laughed again, the bitterness gone, and Roger seemed relieved. He hated confrontation, even when he wasn't directly involved.

"David, if I had any part, even if I might have had a part ... ." He spoke in a low, serious voice. "Well, I can give Amy some money to ... help out."

I thought of all the money Amy could raise from guys who *might have had a part* and almost burst out laughing. I restrained myself, so Roger wouldn't think I was making fun of him.

"Thanks Roger," I said. "That means a lot to me, and I'm sure it will to Amy. Sorry for the interruption."

I knew Roger's offer wouldn't mean jack shit to Amy, but I felt like protecting Roger right then. That's also why I didn't tell him that she wasn't going to keep the baby.

Roger was from St. Francisville, Louisiana, where the main action in town was the arrival and departure of the New Roads ferry. The town's big plantation house held tours for tourists, but when the sun went down, the ferry stopped running, the tourists left, and the inhabitants shut their doors. I doubted Roger had the experience to prepare him for this situation, and I wanted to send him to his chem final thinking everything was okay again.

Besides, I was impressed that Roger was willing to go through this crisis with me. Maybe he was mostly thinking about Amy, but he hadn't walked away from me either. Yeah, despite his glasses and owlish look, Roger was a stand-up guy and a good buddy.

Roger held out his hand, and when I took it, he gave mine a tight squeeze. As he turned to go, I thought about telling him to keep Amy's news to himself, then I decided that his handshake was insurance enough.

I watched Roger walk away, and I found myself envying him, something I had never felt before. I recognized it as another inkling that I was yearning for something that I had openly disdained until recently.

I squashed the feeling and went back into our suite. Roger could walk away, but Amy and I had to settle things here and now. If she was asleep, I would have to wake her up.

9

Amy was awake.

She was sitting on my bed, with her knees drawn up to her chest. Her long hair, more khaki-colored than brown, hung in tangled strands over her forehead, half-concealing her face.

I sat down next to her again, but she moved away from me this time. This made me furious. Hadn't I just spent the last hour comforting her? An hour I could have spent studying to improve my grades and maybe my whole life.

Hadn't I said that I was willing to take responsibility for a mistake that likely wasn't mine? Wasn't I doing

everything a girl in her situation could possibly hope
for?

And she dared to move away from me, on my own
bed, in my own room, as though she didn't need me?

I didn't say any of this to her. I knew that it would
lead to a dead end, and besides, she was already
distressed enough. I drew up my desk chair opposite
her, making it clear that I thought it was time for
a real talk.

Amy stretched out her legs and reached for her
purse. I thought she was going for a cigarette, and
although I knew it was bad to smoke during
pregnancy, I said nothing. I suspected she needed
to calm her nerves. But instead of a pack of cigarettes,
she pulled out the plastic bag of white powder she
had shown me earlier. She opened the bag and
scraped up some of the powder on the tip of one of
her long, press-on fingernails.

I hit her. For the first and last time.

I really only punched her arm, but she was so
unstable that she fell off the bed and onto the floor.
She dropped the bag, and the white powder spilled
out onto the filthy green linoleum.

"Goddamn it, David." Her voice was husky from
crying. She began trying to sweep the powder back
into the bag with the side of her hand.

The thought of what she planned to do not only
to herself, but to what might potentially become a
person made me so angry that I lost control.

The plastic bag was almost full again, and I
wrenched it out her hand. I ran out of the room and
raced down the hall to the bathroom.

"Stop it, David! Stop it!" she yelled, flying after me.

I burst through the bathroom door, surprising Mike Dobbins, who was taking a leak.

"Jesus, David!" Mike turned his head, but he finished pissing. "What the hell ...?"

Mike stopped in midsentence when Amy hurtled through the door. He headed for the door without zipping his pants, sidestepping to avoid running into Amy.

Amy didn't stop rushing at me, but I didn't stop either. I banged into the first cubicle I found and emptied the entire bag into the toilet. Just as the last of the powder settled on the surface of the water, Amy began to pound my back with both fists.

I flushed the toilet, but I didn't dare turn around. I knew Amy would scratch at my face with her long fake nails. Instead, I braced myself and let her hit me and hit me.

"You bastard! You bastard!" she screamed at me. "That wasn't yours. It was mine, goddamn you."

Then she slumped forward against my back, wrapped her arms around me and began sobbing. She gasped for breath between sobs, and I felt her whole body shake.

The entire episode played out in less than five minutes, but with Amy being so upset and me starting out so angry, hours seemed to pass.

I found it difficult to believe that a mere two hours ago I had been blissfully, if uncomfortably, concentrating on Mill and Aristotle and those other dead white males. Now I wondered how studying old books could possibly have anything to do with the life I had stuck myself with.

10

I want to interrupt myself to make clear that I am not telling you all this as a cautionary tale to scare you into taking the straight path. I didn't take that path, and it wasn't the worst decision I ever made. But I can't say it was the best either.

My story isn't like those bullshit films they used to show us in health class about how drugs and sex can fuck up your life and leave you clawing through the trash in the gutter in the hope of finding a joint.

Nor is my story an argument against abortion.

God knows Amy should not have had that child. She really was not a fit mother at that time, if she ever was at any time, and it was for the good of all involved that she did not.

What I'm telling you isn't that anything other than the straight and narrow will screw you over, but how my own choices screwed me. I'm leading up to why Amy left me for what I thought was for good, which I believe had everything to do with that day.

I'm giving you the background you need to understand why the last five years, and the years before them, have been even worse than that first acid trip, with all its paranoid fears and nightmarish images.

11

Amy collapsed against me in the bathroom.

It was as though everything went out of her all at once. She would have fallen to the dingy tile floor, if I hadn't caught her. I scooped her up in my arms and carried her back to my room.

She didn't say a thing. If I had known the word at that time, I would have called her catatonic. I propped her up in my bed, but she still didn't speak. I thought maybe she'd go to sleep, so I pulled up a chair near the window and went back to studying for my exam.

She never seemed to fall asleep, but she didn't speak either. Maybe after two hours, Roger looked in, but he didn't say anything, apparently thinking Amy was asleep and not wanting to wake her.

Shortly afterward, I ran down to the 7-Eleven at the end of the block to get some sandwiches and iced tea. I thought that she would be hungry when she finally snapped out of whatever state she was in.

I plowed on with studying philosophy, which I found especially hard to do, since none of it seemed relevant to my situation anymore.

The giant red ball of the summer sun was low on the horizon and the cicadas were singing their rhythmic, wailing song when Amy finally emerged from her stupor.

"David?" She spoke so softly that I thought I'd imagined it.

"Yes?" I hurried over to her bedside.

"I'm not pregnant anymore ...," she said slowly.

Crazy talk, I thought. Magical thinking, a delusion caused by stress.

"I know you want it that way ...," I began, planning to say something comforting.

"No," Amy cut me off. "I mean I'm really not."

She drew back the sheet.

"Jesus, what is that?" Horrified, I backed away from the bed.

Slick, red blood covered the bottom sheet in a large, irregular blotch that started between Amy's legs. Lumps that looked like clumps of jelly were mixed with the blood, and streaks of blood ran down her legs all the way to her toes.

I was horrified by the blood, but even more shocking was that it was so unexpected. If Amy had been crying or screaming or doubled up with pain, I could have braced myself. But she hadn't so much as spoken for three hours. She had sat quietly while something inside her silently gave way.

"I ... think it's a ... miscarriage." Amy looked completely bewildered.

I felt as confused as Amy looked and didn't know what to think. Was it really a miscarriage, an accident that happened at the most convenient time? And how could she possibly be okay with so much blood pouring out of her body?

I fought the urge to tell her to cover herself up again, so that I didn't have to see what was on the sheets. But if she could stand what had happened to her, I should be able to stand looking at it.

"You didn't ... did you ... *do* anything?"

My question was awkward, and I knew it sounded accusatory, even though I didn't mean for it to be. But fortunately, Amy was too exhausted or confused to take any offence.

"No," she said, shaking her head slowly. "I didn't take pills or shove anything inside me. Not even a drink, which is making this even harder."

I wracked my brain for an explanation. High-school health science didn't help, then I remembered something I overheard my sister's friend Tammy telling her during one of our bus rides to an antiwar demonstration in New Orleans.

"You don't need to go to a clinic or take drugs," Tammy said. "Just get stressed out and fall down the stairs."

Given what Amy and I had been through earlier, that made sense of what was happening now.

"It must have been the stress," I said, finally. "All that emotion and strain. You've been worked up for the past few hours, then I ... ."

I paused, because I found it hard to acknowledge that I'd done anything that had led to the blood soaking my sheets.

"I knocked you off the bed, and you hit the floor hard." I made myself go on. "I feel terrible about that, because I never wanted to do anything to hurt you."

"Forget about that," she cut me off. "I know you don't pull shit like that. But is what you're saying true?"

"I'm pretty sure," I said. I felt a tingle of excitement as I started to recall things I had seen or read. "Lots of characters in books and movies have miscarriages after they fall off horses or tumble downstairs. And a friend of my sister told her she could … ."

"Thanks, Professor," Amy interrupted. She didn't make the title harsh, but she didn't make it sweet either. "But do you have a more biological or scientific reason for what happened?"

"I think so," I said. "Did you ever feel sick before you had to do something you didn't want to do?"

"In the second grade, I threw up every morning before going to school. Is that the kind of thing you mean?"

"Exactly. Stress screws your body, and I'm guessing you've been stressed for … I don't know. How long have you known?"

I wanted to know the answer, but not for scientific reasons.

"Let's see … ." She paused to consider. "I suspected for about three weeks, but I felt sure this last week. Nobody misses two periods without worrying about this." She gave a humorless laugh. "But I guess it's not *this* anymore, is it?"

My mind began to race, because it struck me for the first time that I could still be in trouble, although trouble of a different sort. Amy was seventeen and so still a minor. Could I be arrested for statutory rape? I couldn't see why not. And if Roger or anyone else walked in and saw the blood and decided we had caused the miscarriage ourselves and reported it to the cops…maybe I could also be charged with performing an abortion.

I said nothing about any of this to Amy, but I

decided that getting the mess cleaned up before anybody else happened to come in was a good idea.

"So what do we do now?" Amy asked.

"We clean up." I spoke automatically.

She started laughing, but almost at once it verged on the hysterical. I was afraid she might hyperventilate or even faint.

"But first you need to drink something." I got up from my chair and picked up the paper bag with the iced tea and sandwiches I had bought at the 7-Eleven. "And eat something, if you think you can keep it down. Your body has got to be dehydrated from the blood loss."

I held out a plastic cup of iced tea.

Amy stopped laughing, then looked at the cup of iced tea for a moment. She took it from me, pushed off the lid and began drinking the tea.

"The ice is melted," I said. "But the tea is still cold, and the sugar ought to give you some energy. Do you want to try to eat a cheese sandwich?"

"Later," Amy said. She wiped her mouth with the back of her hand. "But the tea is good."

Amy put the cup down on the floor, stood up, then peeled off her bloody cutoffs. She swiped away a few strands of hair, leaving what could have been a bloody gash across her forehead. My stomach heaved at the sight of so much blood, at the odor of it.

"Go buy me some Kotex," Amy said. "I'm not done bleeding. And stop by Steve Henderson's room and pick up my bag. I need some clothes."

"Okay," I said. "But before I go, have a seat in this chair." I turned the chair so she could get into it more easily. "You could be suffering from shock. Sit here and drink some more iced tea."

"Okay," she agreed. She actually sounded relieved at being told something to do. The experience had to be as unreal for her as for me, maybe even more so for her.

"Back in a second," I said. "I need to get you set up before I go to the store."

I left our suite and walked down the hall to the janitor's closet opposite the communal bathroom. The door was unlocked, and I found the yellow plastic bucket I was looking for. On a narrow shelf above the dirty porcelain slops sink were packages of brown paper towels for the bathroom dispenser. I tucked a package under my arm and was about to close the door when I noticed a large sponge in the sink. I shoved it between my armpit and the paper towels. I glanced around for garbage bags, but I didn't see any.

I filled the yellow bucket half full in one of the shower stalls and took it back to my room.

Amy was still in the chair, looking too exhausted to move. She still held the iced tea, and the clear plastic cup didn't seem to have much left in it. I put the bucket, sponge, and bundle of paper towels on the floor beside the chair.

"Give me one of your hands," I said.

I knelt beside Amy. When she held out her left hand, I took it by the wrist. I then dunked the sponge in the water and wiped the blood off her fingers, then the back and front of her hand. I let the bloody water drip into the bucket.

She switched the cup of iced tea to her left hand so that I could do the same to her right hand. When both her hands were clean, I slid some paper towels out of the package and dried them off.

"Okay," I said. "I'm going to go buy the Kotex, and while I'm gone, try to eat a sandwich. One is plain cheese, and the other is pimento cheese. Does either sound good?"

"Maybe I can handle the plain cheese," Amy said. "I do feel kind of weak."

"Blood loss can cause shock," I said, repeating half of what I had said earlier.

I got the cheese sandwich from the paper bag, unwrapped it, and handed Amy one of the halves. She took it, but did nothing but hold it, as if unsure that she could hold down any food.

Before I left, I had a final thought. I got my maroon terrycloth bathrobe out of my closet and draped it over Amy's shoulders.

"It's going to get bloody," she said.

"That won't show," I said. "Besides, I don't care. You need to stay warm, because of the shock."

I knew about shock from my Boy Scout first-aid training, and even though it must have been ninety degrees in the room, I thought that Amy might still get chilled.

"Don't try to do anything until I get back," I told her. "Here's the other iced tea. Drink it if you can." I put the cup and the other half of the sandwich on the floor beside her chair. "I'm not going to run away," Amy said. "Not that I have any place to run to anyway."

12

The 7-Eleven was only a block away, so it didn't take more than fifteen minutes to buy the Kotex and a roll of black plastic garbage bags. I also picked up a six-pack of cold Cokes. In the south, Coke is like a medicine, and I thought the sugar and caffeine might help Amy's recovery.

I wasn't looking forward to dealing with Steve. He was a management trainee at a Sears store and considered himself superior to ordinary *college boys*, as he called us. He had a profound dislike of anyone he suspected might be smarter than him, and given that his IQ was lower than his shoe size that meant nearly everybody.

I got lucky, though. Steve wasn't home, and his roommate handed over Amy's small, blue-denim duffle bag without comment.

When I walked into my room, Amy was right where I'd left her, sitting on the chair beside the bed.

If this were a story in a magazine, it would make more sense if I were able to say that, while I was gone, Amy walked out of my life. But this is not a piece of magazine fiction, and my life doesn't read like a story would.

"How are you feeling?" I asked.

I noticed that she had stuffed the pillowcase between her legs to stop the blood she said was still oozing out of her. I wondered if I shouldn't take her to a hospital to get a transfusion. If I stayed with her, I was likely to get into trouble, but that would be better than letting her die.

"Better," she said. She clutched the collar of the maroon bathrobe, holding it shut. "I ate the cheese sandwich and finished the tea. That helped. You were right."

"How about a Coke?"

I pulled loose a plastic bottle from the six-pack and twisted off the cap. I held it out to her. If she didn't want it, I would drink it myself.

She accepted the bottle and took a long drink. As with the tea, she wiped her mouth with the back of her hand.

"That tastes great," she said. "I think I might live."

"Feel strong enough to make it to the shower?"

"Oh, yeah. I'm ready, even if you have to carry me."

"Stay where you are for a minute," I said. "I'll see if the coast is clear."

Before I left, I got a large blue bath towel, a matching washcloth, a plastic bottle of shampoo, and a bar of Dove soap out of my bureau drawers. I stuffed everything except the towel in the paper bag with the Kotex, then I picked up Amy's denim duffle and walked down the hall to the bathroom.

I pushed open the bathroom door and took a quick glance around. The doors to the toilets were open and the curtains on the two shower stalls were pulled back. Nobody.

I wasn't surprised. Because it was exam period, most people would be studying in the library to take advantage of the air conditioning. Roger and I were the oddballs.

I hung the towel on the rack by the first shower stall and put the washcloth, soap, and bottle of shampoo on the shelf inside. I left the bag with the Kotex and the duffel bag on the metal bench in front of the showers.

Then I went back for Amy.

While I stood by the door to keep out anybody who happened to try to come in, Amy showered, washed her hair, and dressed in jeans and a blue LSU T-shirt that she took out of her duffle bag. I assumed she also used the Kotex, but I didn't ask her.

We managed to get back to my room without running into anybody.

"Sit at my desk and have another Coke, while I clean up," I told her. "There's another sandwich, pimento cheese."

"I can help," she said. "I'm not a cripple."

"I know you're not," I said. "But you still have some recovering to do, and besides, the clean-up isn't that much, really."

"I'm sorry about your sheets. Could they be bleached?"

"I'm not going to try to wash them," I said. "I've got another set, and I can buy more."

Amy didn't raise any more objections, which made me think that she was still feeling a little weak. She sat at my desk with a bottle of Coke and the pimento cheese sandwich. I turned the fan so that it was blowing on her. With her wet hair hanging down and her scrubbed face, I was taken with how pretty she looked and by how young she was.

I stripped off the top sheet and stuffed it into a black garbage bag. Averting my eyes from the gelatinous mass on the bed, I folded up the bottom sheet, starting from the top, then stuffed it into the same bag. The pillowcase that Amy had put between her legs had so much blood on it that it clearly wasn't worth trying to save. It went into the same bag.

The blue-and-white ticking of the mattress was stained right in the center, but that was mostly all the damage. I knew I couldn't clean it up completely, but I wiped off as much blood as I could with the sponge. The dark red became sort of pink. Then I turned the mattress over, hiding the stained part.

I wiped down the chair beside the bed, the one Amy had been sitting in. The T-shirt she had used to stop her bleeding went into the bag.

I tackled the floor next. Most of the blood had stayed on the sheets, and only a few dribbles and smears were beside the bed. I got down on my knees, and after a few wide sweeps with the big sponge, the green linoleum around the bed soon looked cleaner than the rest of the floor. The water in the green bucket wasn't so much red anymore as dirty rust color.

I pulled tight the ties on the plastic garbage bag and secured them with a square knot. I had been thinking about how suspicious I would look if I met up with people on the stairs while taking the bag to the dumpster behind the building. The solution I came up with was simple and, I thought, elegant.

The rear window in my room was directly above the parking lot where the dumpster was located. I dragged the bag over to the window, unfastened the screen, pushed it up, then stuck my head out to check if anyone was in the parking lot. I saw nobody.

So I heaved the bag up to the window sill and shoved it out. The bag made a solid plop as it hit the concrete three stories below.

"I'm going to go empty this bucket, then go downstairs and throw that bag into the dumpster," I told Amy.

"I feel bad about not helping," she said.

"Just get your strength back." I picked up the bucket and opened the door. "That's the most important way to help."

Just as I stepped out into the hall, I saw Mike, who lived in the suite at the other end of the hall, coming up the stairs.

"Is that part of your Janitorial Science final," he asked, even before he got to the landing.

"The lab part," I said. "Plus a girlfriend who doesn't like stepping on my dirty floor."

"The things we do for love," he said, grinning.

I emptied the yellow bucket in the slop sink, then ran the water and used the sponge to clean it out. I rinsed out the bucket and squeezed out the sponge. I put the sponge where I had found it in the sink. I had the almost fanatical idea that I didn't want to leave a trace of what I had done.

Going down the stairs, I passed no one. The parking lot was still empty. I grabbed the garbage bag by the neck and dragged it across the concrete to the dumpster. Glancing around, I saw no one. I threw the bag into the dumpster.

And then it was done. No more mess, no more baby.

13

My room looked normal again, except for the lack of sheets on the bare mattress.

Amy also looked normal. No one would ever know what we had just been through ... no one except for us.

I twisted open another bottle of Coke and swallowed almost half of it in one long gulp. I was thirsty, and I was hungry. Amy unwrapped the pimento cheese sandwich I had put on the desk and handed me a half. I began nibbling the crust.

Then I broke into tears.

Male sensitivity wasn't in fashion yet, and a man crying was still thought of as weakness personified. Crying in front of Amy was something I never expected to do. I felt disgusted with myself, and I expected her to have the same reaction. But she didn't even seem surprised.

I don't know what came over me there in that stifling room, with the metallic odor of blood still lingering in the air. Looking back, if I wanted to make myself look better, I could say that it was the thought of losing what could have become my child that prompted my tears. But honestly, that wasn't it. I hadn't known about the baby long enough for that to be it. And I hadn't even known if it was mine.

I was crying not for Amy or the baby-to-be, but for myself. I realized with the blinding clarity of a flash of lightning that I wasn't going to have the future that I wanted. I didn't see how anybody could wake up in bed and not know if the blood was theirs or someone else's and go on to be successful. I didn't see how anybody could be involved in a do-it-yourself abortion and put it behind him so completely that he could go on with the life that he had planned. I felt, at the time, that the only path open to me was one leading to the gutter. The idea of becoming a professor now seemed on a par with the silly ideas that children have when they say they want to be a fireman or an astronaut. So I was crying not for Amy or the baby-to-be, but for myself. At the most basic level, we're all selfish and egocentric, and anyone who tells you different is either lying or too optimistic for his own good.

The crying didn't last long. Somehow, I was more afraid that Roger or some other guy might come in and find me bawling than I had been of them seeing bloodstains. Unlike tears, blood was intimidating, impressive, and made me slightly dangerous. I choked down my tears, and Amy held my hand until my sobs finally subsided.

Neither of us spoke. We each stared off into space, avoiding making eye contact. I thought I could smell the pimento in my half-eaten sandwich over the lingering scent of blood.

Suddenly, Amy got out of her chair, picked up her blue-denim duffle bag and started for the door.

"Where are you going?" I asked, startled.

"Out of here," she answered.

"Wait a minute," I said. "At least take the Kotex."

I realized the moment I said it, how absurd it sounded. But I wasn't able to make sense of anything at that time.

Amy turned and snatched up the brown paper bag with the box of Kotex. She walked out of my room, and I could hear the door to the suite close behind her.

The unfairness hit me hard.

I had told her I would take care of her, accept a child that might not even be mine, and marry her, if that's what she wanted. I had cradled her, watched over her, and stroked her hair while she was upset. I had done my best to keep her from going into shock. I had cleaned her up and taken care of all the mess.

And she couldn't even spend the rest of the goddamn night with me?

I felt a hot anger spread through me. But I wasn't just furious, I was confused. Amy was a dangerous girl to love, a heartbreaker. I knew about the danger, because she had warned me. But I thought I was special, and I was just realizing, that made me blind to the risk.

I began to cry again, almost silently. Eventually, I dried my eyes and wiped my face with the bunched-up tail of my T-shirt. I hadn't heard Roger come in and decided he must have found somewhere else to spend the night. I glanced at the clock on my desk and saw that it was past midnight.

I had a philosophy final in less than nine hours.

I didn't go to that final.

I didn't go to any of my finals. I took off for home before school even ended, earning incompletes in all my classes. I felt that I was following the path fate had set for me. But I really wasn't. At the time, I was too upset and too goddamn furious to realize that it wasn't fate setting my path. I was doing it all by myself.

I lost my scholarship, and that meant I lost my chance to finish college. But that last part is probably a lie. Chances are that, with some self-discipline and determination, I could have finished my incompletes over the summer, then saved up enough money to enroll at least part-time in the fall semester.

I was too busy making myself into a martyr even to try. Instead, I got a job at Sunshine Realtors as a sort of gopher. I went out to put up or take down signs, delivered contracts, chauffeured clients to properties, and when necessary, swept floors or washed windows in vacant properties before they were shown. Eventually, I was promised, I could get a real-estate license and be taken on as a trainee.

The job was easy, but completely uninteresting. Still, it was a respectable job and paid what I thought was a reasonable salary. I earned enough to get my own apartment.

But most of this story has to do with Amy, not me.

Like I said before, Amy didn't leave for good that night. That would have made sense, but she didn't leave me at any time that made sense.

Before I left, I packed up one of the black garbage bags with all of the clothes, shoes, and makeup that she had stored in my room, and at some point, she picked it up from Roger. She hung round the university for a while, bumming food and shelter and whatever else she needed from the boys she'd met there.

She left before any of them guessed that she might not be pregnant anymore. My guess is that she had lived off guilt and sympathy and a bit of fear for about as long as she could.

I'm not sure how she knew where I lived, but she came to see me that July. It was almost, but not quite, a year to the day since we first met at Joe Conway's party.

I was eating a typical bachelor's dinner: cold ravioli right out of a can, with a few beers to wash it down. In those days, a few really meant a few, and my drinking was pretty restrained. It didn't start for real until Amy came back.

I lived in another third-floor walk-up, without air conditioning, of course. It was the life we were all used to. I had my door and all my windows open that night, trying to get a cross-breeze going. That's how, as I was sitting at my table with a Reader's Digest open in front of me, Amy was able to just walk right in.

I looked up, so surprised that for an instant I didn't recognize her. Red tomato sauce was dripping down my chin, and I wiped it off with a corner of the magazine.

Amy walked into my narrow kitchenette and began opening cabinets, glancing inside, then shutting them.

"Don't you have anything fit to eat?" she asked. She addressed the question to an open cabinet.

I felt torn between telling her off for breezing in after three months of ignoring me and getting up and finding her something she might want to eat. I found myself staring at her lithe body, noticing how her short white skirt barely covered her rounded ass.

Then I stood up to find her something to eat.

"I, uh, don't keep much food here," I said, walking over to stand beside her. "I don't … entertain … often."

She detected my sarcasm and turned her head to look at me. She had cut off some of her hair, so that it now hung just below her shoulders, instead of down her back. She walked past me to get to the next cabinet, and when her hair brushed my arm, a tingle as real as an electrical charge ran through my body.

"Don't be like that," she said. She grabbed a box of Cheerios off the shelf and sat down at the table. "I'm not going to bother you for long."

"Why are you here at all?" I asked, leaning on the counter.

"Oh, for this and that," she said. She waved a hand vaguely, as though that helped illustrate her point.

"Does *this and that* mean you'll be around town now? At Joe's maybe?"

I knew that sounded harsh, but I couldn't help it.

Amy stared at me for a very long minute, making clear she wasn't going to dignify the question with a response. Dropping her gaze, she began popping Cheerios into her mouth, one by one.

"I'll be around," she said, not looking at me.

"And where exactly is that?" My tone was nasty. "Have you been able to sucker somebody into letting you stay with them? If that's why you came here, remember that I'm not as easy to manipulate as some people. I know you too well and have seen you do it too often." I shook my head. "I'm sick of being played. Eat some cereal, drink a beer if you want it. Then get the hell out of here."

I didn't add that she had hurt me more than she could ever understand when she had walked out of my dorm room. I had accepted her comings and goings, and it wasn't as if I had simply bought her dinner from time to time. Or that we had been buddies having a few drinks before bed. Nothing between us had been casual or ordinary, and I had expected that the experiences we had shared would mean something to her.

Her walking out meant that it didn't. And this is what made me feel something beyond hurt and disappointment and despair. Even though the metaphor is fraught with irony, I felt as if she had raped me, then tossed me aside.

I had learned in my LSU English Lit class that *rape* comes from a Latin word for *seize* or *snatch*, and originally, even in English, it didn't have anything to do with sex.

That's how Amy made me feel—like she had snatched something from me. I couldn't say what she had snatched. It couldn't be innocence, because I wasn't innocent when I met her. I think what she had taken from me was my expectations.

Before she walked out, I had been able to expect good things to happen. In my mind, studying, partying, getting to know people, all added up to a ticket to a life better than any I had known. I didn't merely want a better life, I expected it.

But when Amy passed through that door and left me alone in my room that expectation shattered like a dropped mirror. I lost my faith in the future, and almost immediately, my life became empty and meaningless. I suffered the same fate that, ironically, I had predicted for Amy.

But, as matters turned out, I wasn't wrong on that count.

14

Amy reacted to my outburst with nothing more than a bored expression. She continued to pop Cheerios into her mouth.

I stared at her with an angry expression. Each crunch of cereal sounded like a small explosion in my ears. I fought the impulse to wrench the box away from her and throw it against the wall.

How could she not understand how serious I was?

She closed the flaps on the Cheerios box, walked over to the kitchenette, and returned the box to its place in the cabinet. She then turned to face me.

"Okay, David," she said. "I'll stay somewhere else, and I won't bother you again."

I said nothing as I watched her walk out the door she had so recently breezed through. My resolve lasted only until I heard her feet on the stairs. I ran after her.

I wanted to tell her that I really hadn't meant what I said. I wanted to apologize for my harshness and plead with her to come back. I wanted to tell her that I was sure she had her reasons for walking out on me that night. Maybe reasons I would never—could never—understand.

I wanted to smooth over everything, make everything okay, and make her mine. I wanted to start over from square one, back where there were no cocaine highs, no battles over how she behaved, no wide-eyed stares from Roger, no babies, no bloody sheets, and most of all, no icy void where my heart should be.

I stumbled onto the landing and leaned over the railing.

"Amy!" I yelled down to her. She had reached only the second floor, but she didn't answer. She was not, in any sense, my girl the way Stella was in *Streetcar*, when Marlon Brando yelled for her.

15

That was the night that I drank myself unconscious for the first time ever.

I didn't want to think anymore. I wanted to slip into a welcoming, soft oblivion and never emerge. I wanted two incompatible things: to live without Amy and to live without pain.

She left Melville either that night or the next day. I have no way of knowing. She slipped out of our town and out of my life. Back then, in the Seventies, it was easier for people to do that. E-mail didn't exist, and no one had a cell phone. If people didn't tell you what town they were living in, didn't give you an address, and maybe didn't even have a telephone, when it came to locating them, you were pretty much stuck. That was particularly true of Amy; she never really had an address.

But Amy didn't disappear forever.

She didn't show up again until February of 1981, almost four years after she walked out on me for the second time. True to form, even after so much time had passed, she had not lost her capacity to surprise me.

She showed up, out of the blue, and knocked on my door.

Jared 2002

I actually lost.

We played Rock paper scissors the way we did with everything we disputed, from whose chocolate bar it really was, to who had to give Jen a bath this morning, to who got to kick Darrin Burlington's ass on the playground that day.

But that time we played for much, much more.

One two three shoot.

I think about that a lot as I go from day to day the subway rushing by me the people rushing by me everyone rushing rushing rushing in a hurry to be wherever whenever.

In this city time is king, and his minions hurry to and fro, always wondering, worrying Am I late or are you late? or What time is it? Is the train late? Is traffic bad? Should we bother with a taxi or walk? And you know, in all that traffic, there's not a single *pickup truck.*

That's where it happened, sitting in the back of the pickup it must have been five years ago by now when we were really just boys could barely drive the damn pickup and yet here we were sitting face to face and I could see the look on his and knew it was probably on mine looking more like twins than we even did normally and we had our hands bunched into fists like we were about to start going at each other like in the playground fights or the ones he still had in junior high when he went that is.

All these faces and not one of them familiar.

It's haunting in a way that with all the people rushing and pushing and shoving, more people than were in my school class all bunched into a single subway car, and not a single one of them is ever anyone you recognize; it's never someone you think it would be. People, people, people the streets are thick with people, and the buildings are filled with them, and yet with all those people, there's never the one you want to see and never even the one you don't, just anonymous people, people rushing and bustling and taking no notice of you whatsoever, because that's the way of the city, and you'll just never bump into

him

sitting cross legged atop the cooler we had in those days and me kneeling and eyeing each other with anxiety since it was really it this time we had to find a compromise and one of us had to go and as he sat there and looked at me and got ready to throw ... scissors was it? Or maybe rock? Whatever it was it beat me good that time both times because I actually lost that time but sitting there with hair flopping into his face he looked so much like

"Daddy? Daddy, why is there a track in the middle? The train can't let anyone on if it stops in the middle!"

"That's because the train that goes on that track doesn't stop here. It's for the express train, you know, the Two and Three?"

"Oh right. It doesn't stop until 96th Street."

That kid can't be more than five and already knows the subways like a pro. City kids like that just kill me, really, because they seem too young to know all that they do and to have been exposed to so many things I'll bet the same kid wouldn't flinch at being grabbed by a homeless person the way I flinched back four years ago when I first got to this city and, like so many others, had no idea that it was just a way of life, just something you knew, like express trains and locals and the MTA and the LIRR and uptown and downtown and crosstown and FDR Drive and Henry Hudson Parkway and West Side Highway and the Triboro bridge. It was life and it was, city life, and this kid would be lucky enough to always know, and if he was really fortunate lucky enough to always have a

"Daddy? Where's Daddy?"

Her face was honestly bewildered and it was up to one of us to tell her because she was only three years old but even at three your family owes you some honesty and Mom was obviously not going to do it because she was busy calling everyone at the office and the bar and Grandma's house calling calling calling and getting the same answer in the same tone all of which implied that

"You must have known this was coming." Not a question but a statement, and he directed it right at me. I opened my mouth to tell him of course I hadn't, but the words got wrapped around my tongue, so I didn't say anything coherent, just stared back at him. Some big brother I was; I was supposed to be able to hold the family together and comfort them and pull together through hard times, and here I was face to face with a little brother who dealt with reality and everything else better than I ever had. When I think about that, then sometimes I wonder if it was for that reason rather than the one he gave that

One two three shoot.

Nails ragged and dirty, because we'd pitched a tent in the backyard as a kind of game for the kids, and we watched them run in and out of it. Well, watched two of them. She was sitting off to the side, as she always did, maybe waiting for a boy, because she seemed to spend most of her life from twelve on waiting for some boy. To me, that day, she didn't look like she should be waiting for one. Her legs were gawky and thin, sticking out from her cutoff shorts, and her elbows stuck out, sharp as ice picks. Her hair was over her face, hiding it from the world, and she didn't look pretty at all. Didn't look sexy at all, just looked young as hell and hurt and scared, and it made me furious as I looked across the yard and saw that some dumbass from junior frickin' high school was about to meet up with her. When she was just a kid, just a frightened little girl

I want nothing but for you both to leave me the hell alone! Quit trying to be him! You're not him! Neither of you are and neither of you have the right to tell me the things you're telling me.

Quit acting like you can do this when you're only two years older and not much better. You think I don't know about Rosetta and all those others? If you

can do it, if Mom can do it, so can I. So don't you dare think you can try and stop me.

Boy, she was a fireball, a regular pit bull when you made her mad. I hated to be around her and hated to fight with her, but he would always take her on, no matter what she threw at him, because all the stuff about girls really was for him, not me. As much alike as we looked, somehow they all fell hard for him and ignored me.

Some frickin' older brother.

I stood there while he took her on and tried to win her over, and she hurled insult after insult right at him, until he said he loved her too much to see this happen to her and she practically spat in his face at that and asked if he wouldn't like a turn then... .

That never had a sister.

But I don't love her like that, like Quentin, and neither did he. But she treated us that way, because we were men and we were like that of course. Didn't we see it day after day even before Dad left she would add with fire in her eyes and I would quail while he went right up against her, right up to her gaze and insults and sometimes I honestly felt that he knew how much more suited he was than I was, though he never rubbed it in my face ... but all the same.

One two three shoot.

I could see all those dirty nails because that first time it was paper that's what it was and I threw rock because I always thought of that as the hardest to beat since it could smash those damn scissors but

*then again as everyone knows Paper Wraps Rock he
was very quiet when he said it and we went through
the motions solemnly as though it weren't a kids'
game we were playing and of course it wasn't, not at
this point because it wasn't just a Hershey bar at
stake here.*

That never had a sister.

I remember when I discovered that book for the
first time and the feeling it gave me it wasn't just
that it was like the calculus of literature a kind of
reading that took all my concentration and all my
thought and required that I piece the puzzle together
it was the echo I found of myself and my family and
the feeling that just maybe we weren't as screwed
up as I always thought we had been and maybe
someone else somewhere understood besides the
obvious one who did

No Harvard for me though it's close I pace other
hallowed halls of learning and sit in ancient
classrooms I study ancient texts and think about
how ancient families are even more fucked up than
mine and that makes me feel a little better and as
I think about that I also think about how no one
here knows who I am or where I'm from and how I
wouldn't even be here if it weren't for financial aid
and scholarships and very rich alums who want to
feel that they've made the world a better place for
some people at least

But only those with the proper SAT scores and
teacher recs at least that's what they said when I
said I wanted to apply but then I kept pressing it
kept talking about how that implied that everyone

was lucky enough to have a real family and a real high school and teachers who give a shit what happens to the kids they've known when real life doesn't work that way and real life is what I've lived and I think they believed my case because here I am either that or they got too damn scared that they'd get sued for discrimination if they refused me for that reason so I'm here and here I've been for the past 18 months.

Sometimes I get to thinking my life is hard because I have to study all the time to even reach a par with all the kids here because most of them came from good schools good homes good families at least that's what it seems like but maybe they are hiding something too maybe they're more like me than I'll ever know but as of right now I don't know and I just feel like I'm fighting to even keep up with those prep school educations.

Sometimes I get to thinking my life is hard when I have tests and papers on the same day and I've had to work my job the night before and I think how I'm too tired to piece together what the similarities are between Socrates in Plato's *Symposium* and Dionysus in Euripides' *The Bacchae* or to discuss the rise and fall of Rome or Caesar Augustus' relationship to the Biblical accounts of history, days when I'm too tired to conjugate another Latin verb or to theorize why mitochondria retain their own DNA and the ability to live as separate organisms, days when I feel sorry for me in this cold unfeeling city and wish for the rolling plains of home.

And then I realize what a hard life is.

Plains rolling sure but when I heard from Grandma three years ago they are rolling past the windows of the pickup for Mom and Tommy and Sarah and Jen and Will and Casey stretch out in the back and pray that there won't be an accident or maybe they pray that there will be

I wish I were dead. I really do. I kept my eyes shut because I knew this was not something I was meant to hear and that if I revealed I'd been awake she'd shut up for sure but I could hear and I heard him shift up in the bed next to mine heard her sit down gingerly on the edge heard him sit up and place his arms around her and heard her start to cry quietly and for a while there was nothing but her crying and the soft whisper of his hand rubbing against her nylon nightshirt then

Why don't you wish he were? Why you? You didn't do anything none of us did all of this in soft anger so that I wouldn't wake and interrupt but the emotion was too much to contain to whispers and he got louder if anyone should die it should be him for leaving us like this and for making you ... making me ... making Jared and Mom and all the rest wish that ... wanted to and I heard her crawl in and curl up beside him and heard both of them cry together in the bed holding each other together

That never had a sister.

I wanted more than anything to open my eyes and cry out and crawl in and hold and be held and I cried too to my pillow but I didn't open my eyes and I didn't intrude because he was always better at it than I was and always knew what was right to say

so that even when they fought and fought and fought they'd end up together and end up on each other's side and it was that more than the hair and eyes and the very occasional smile that made me think of Dad and the way he could handle her and handle all of us

Some big brother.

I slept eventually like always and she was gone when I got up and he was just getting up and I looked at him and maybe expected him to say something or do something and I guess he could read me cause he always could read me better than I read him and he paused with his shirt half on and said "Soon. We have to pick soon."

One two three ...

I often wonder if anyone was watching that day but why should they since it didn't look like we were doing anything different from normal but the way we were staring at each other it wasn't like prizefighters or anything but it sure wasn't friendly it was too intense to be friendly and I felt his eyes boring into me and mine into his because in a lot of ways we were the same though never the Camden twins like people called us sometimes and it wasn't true either that we could read each other's minds he could just read mine because he was like that he was that way Will was

SHOOT

The second time it was paper again for him and I'd thrown scissors because somehow I knew he would do it again so I won that time so it was even it was down to the final round to the last chance it all came down to this.

Will licked his lips which were cracking in the heat and wiped a hand across his brow it came away muddy because a fine film of dust had settled over us when we were pitching the tent sweat dripped off my brow and I did the same copying him a weak imitation as always some big brother...

He kept holding my gaze. *You sure you wanna?* I guess ... don't you? *I don't know ... maybe we do better together What if you leave and it all goes to hell* What he meant was what if he left and it all went to hell as it probably would have and I knew he meant it then and I know he meant it now but what I didn't know was that whether he stayed or left whether I went on or kept up it was all going anyway.

SHOOT

The third time I threw rock.

I figured it was my best bet because if he threw scissors I won and if he threw rock we went again and I'd only lose if he threw paper which he'd just done twice so he couldn't possibly throw paper

He threw paper. And I lost. I actually lost that time.

It was Will who was to leave. Will who was to get out of this town and go find himself somewhere better and something better to do Will who didn't have to live day in and day out with the family and who might go on to be something better than we had been and I felt jealous and sad but even more than that I felt really really worried because Some big brother ... yeah that was me ...

He looked at me then as we both withdrew our hands as though we'd stuck them in a furnace we wiped them off on the seats of our jeans because in all that tension and clenching they'd gotten all sweaty and I "I guess that's all" and he "So it's settled" and I "When do you want to leave" and he "No, I mean, it's settled"

And the way he looked at me I knew what he meant and he never said anything else no big speech about why I should go and he should stay he just held out his hand to shake this time and said you'll do better out there than I would.

Some big brother, huh? I just let my little brother take the fall for me the same way I let him take care of the kids and take care of Mom and he really was the older brother except that he was ten months younger than I was so it was settled.

Settled down to the click of the screen porch and the soft crunch of gravel under my feet as I walked off in the night to who knows where and settled to the muffled squeak of springs on the old mattress I was sleeping on with Will and then I walked out of the bedroom glancing in on my sisters all piled up in a heap of three and not one of them stirred and then I heard someone move and I walked faster and quieter because I didn't want it to be any of them and I didn't want it to be Will and I certainly didn't want it to be

"Tommy! Kid, what are you doing? You've got to get back in bed, little man, it's late!" God only knows how he got out here I guess it just goes to show you what a close watch Mom always kept on all of us that my two-year-old brother wandered downstairs and into the kitchen and could have just wandered

out the screen door the way his older brother was about to do but there he was in nothing but a Huggies diaper with his too-long hair curling around his face and looking like one of those plaster angels that decorate the trailers of people like me people like us who go in for that type of Precious Moments stuff and his hair curled around his face and his huge eyes looked at me uncomprehendingly and I looked back just as bewildered and then

"Tommy! You shouldn't be up!" He was there like always of course he was awake he knew I was to go tonight and had heard the springs squeak and had made them squeak on his own and now we were standing in the kitchen all the men of the family who were left gathered around the screen door and sleepy Tommy stared at both of us and held his arms out to Will who scooped him up and I knew that he'd be taking him back to bed with him because Casey wasn't the only one of us who sought out Will and I would have done it too if I had been any of them

Some big brother.

I started towards both of them because I wanted to kiss Tommy goodbye and hug Will too and he knew that was on my mind but he backed away with his bare foot scuffing the linoleum gently and I noticed then that his feet were too big for the rest of him and that you could almost see his ribs through the Hanes undershirt he had on and Tommy was pressed against those ribs almost asleep again and they both looked tiny both looked so young which of course they were Will was only fifteen still because his birthday was next week and I was just sixteen myself and I'd never felt quite so young as when my little brother holding my baby brother backed away from me and shook his head and I understood that there was no time for risks like that if I wanted to get out and I did so I stared at them and raised my hand a bit and walked out of the screen door and it clicked shut softly on the scene behind me and as I gave one final glance back I saw that it was a real tableau now with Mary and Joseph Casey and Will and little baby Tommy with two smaller fair-haired angels clinging close as well

I actually lost that day.

My boots crunched in the gravel and I was crying by the time I got down the driveway and I kept thinking real men don't cry but I wasn't a man I was a boy I was sixteen I was alone I'd left my family and I was running away from home with my clothes in a paper bag that didn't even have handles and I was scared and I thought then that I was doing the hard thing that running endlessly was going to be the hard thing that sleeping on unfamiliar couches or on park benches and being yelled at by the police and taking charity whenever it was offered even though it went against my instincts and not showering for more than a week and being called all kinds of names when really I was just a scared little boy I thought that was going to be the hard part of it all and I told myself I was glad to be the one going through it instead of Will because I was protecting him I was

Some big brother.

I spent the first day walking through a town where everyone recognized me but no one found it odd that

I was out on my own with a paper bag clutched to me and tear tracks in the red film on my face because that Mississippi dust can really cover you and I saw some knowing looks cross faces and I wondered if they knew that it shouldn't be me walking on the road out of town it should have been him because I actually lost that day I actually lost that day I actually

One two three
SHOOT
SHOOT
SHOOT
Shot

The word was small and spidery and short and I wondered how the word that ended their lives ended mine ended his could possibly be so short but even in that four-letter word worse than any I'd ever used before I sensed my grandmother's hurt and the despair that must be sweeping my family over the brother who was supposed to stay no matter what.

I wish I were dead. I really do. His arm around her shoulder rubbing it with a soft sound and her hair covering his shoulders too bony to be real he held her as I lay in the next bed wishing to hold her wishing to hold him wishing they would both hold me as he said in delicate dangerous fury, *Why don't you wish he were? Why you? You didn't do anything. None of us did. If anyone should be dead, it should be him for leaving us.*

He held her and it was what she wanted to hear and she knew, I felt her knowing, that as long as Will lived on and Will survived she could do it too as long as this champion of a brother kept going and kept loving she could do the same and that her heart would always belong not to the boys who shared her bed and her body but to the boy who shared her mind and her heart and wrapped his thin arms around her frail frame and convinced her that despite their weakness they would endure together.

If anyone should be dead, it should be him for leaving us.

I walked through the night because for some reason I could not stand to stay anywhere where anyone knew who I was. I didn't even want to know who I was because I was the kind of boy who would leave his younger brother the hard work as he went on to save himself I was the kind of man who would leave his family

I was as bad as my father.

No. I was worse.

I was worse because I *understood* my father. I knew that he must have felt as torn and conflicted as I did and that he must have told himself as I did pacing the very same steps he may have taken that they would do better on their own and that they didn't need him really he was just dragging them down that we would do better and Mom would do better without him the way I thought Will would do better without me not realizing that two parents two brothers are always better than just one no matter what the second one is like and that leaving is a selfish act not for anyone's good but my own his own our own

Shot

The safety clicked out of place and I stared at him totally shocked because I didn't know how to fire a real gun just a BB gun but here was Will with a pistol in hand leveling it at Benjy Magee who was better than thirty and Will and I were both just fifteen and Will barely that and we hadn't thrown yet and I hadn't lost yet and it was before that day in the pickup Will was leveling the gun at Benjy Magee and Benjy had a knife to Casey and Casey was staring wide-eyed at Will silently screaming but frozen in fear

Everyone was a part of the scene but me and I just stood by helplessly watching as Will leveled the gun at Benjy and Casey pleaded silently with Will and Benjy looked surly in a drunken stupor and time stood still and I was watching and I saw Will's finger squeeze and felt the sound of the gun before I heard it go off felt it in the deepest part of my stomach and heard the bullet whiz past Benjy heard its deadly tune and realized that was a real

Shot

And that he had deliberately missed. Benjy realized it too drunk as he was he saw in Will's eyes and his aim that the bullet could easily have hit him square between the eyes and that's when Casey screamed and screamed and screamed and I thought it would never stop and flinched but didn't move didn't do anything

Some big brother.

While Will just looked at Benjy and the gun clicked again and I wondered if he would actually pull that trigger another time and this time aim better and I for one didn't want to find out but neither did Benjy and so he dropped Casey like a hot iron and hightailed it out of our yard and Casey was still screaming and Tommy was crying and the girls had started yelling and God almighty where was Mom where was Dad I kept looking around for someone else but not Will he threw the gun on the porch and ran and picked up Casey like she was Sarah and walked to the swing and held her as she cried.

The kids were still crying inside and it occurred to me to get them so I turned around and went in the front door and Jen was holding them on the couch so that they were all just sniffing so I sat down with them and then I thought of the gun on the porch so I went to pick it up but heard Casey murmuring to Will and didn't want to intrude so I sat down in the doorway and began to cry.

Shot

I was putting socks into my paper bag even though I knew changing socks would soon be the least of my worries when he laid his hand on my shoulder and I turned slightly and there was the gun.

"Take it," he said simply and I shook my head at him but he just said "Go on, you never know what you'll find out there."

And I shook my head again unable to think how to explain to him that it was more important that he have it for what he found here and that I didn't even know how to shoot it and that I'd never have cause to use it the way he had and how could I ever follow up that act with anything so I just said "no it's too heavy" and he understood what I meant and took it back and I left it there with him I left it with him

I left him the gun.

I wrote when I had somewhere to write from and wondered why I never heard back, that is until Grandma wrote me to tell me that they had taken off in that old pickup where I actually lost they'd all taken off and I knew how it was then knew how it would always be for them and that's when I first started to realize that I hadn't taken the hard path in leaving but had given him the hard path in staying

Some big brother.

If anyone should be dead, it should be him for leaving us.

Would they want that would they want me dead do I want me dead? After all I did leave them and I remember Will saying that about Dad when Casey came into our room and said so desperately and so truly that she wished she were dead and Will convinced her that she didn't mean that even though he knew as well as I did that she actually did mean it but he made her not believe it because he was so honest and so true and loving and I think he said it not because he really meant it but because it was what she needed to hear to keep living and keep wanting to.

Will did not want Dad dead he would have wished himself dead before any one of us and it looks as though that's what he actually did and so I know I know I know that he wouldn't want me dead because even though I actually lost that day my little brother gave me my life

But even that doesn't do him justice my little brother traded his life for mine and now at the last stage of the trade I have to use my life to do what he would have wanted and do what he could not quite do on his own. I have to use the life he gave me the way he would have me use it I can't keep walking away I am not my father and it took Will's death to make me realize that.

I am not my father and I can do it I can use the life he gave me for someone besides me I can use it for him for her for all of them. I am not my father and I can use my life to go home.

I am going home.

Will 2002

I am far from perfect.

When Jared and I were younger, I used to steal the cookies out of his lunch sack and make him eat my apple for me. When we were older, I used to take what few girlfriends he had (as though I didn't have enough of my own). I lost my virginity at the age of fourteen (she was a wizened fifteen). In my nineteen years I've slept with more than nineteen girls, yet I've never had a girlfriend.

I've broken a good many hearts.

It seems there's something in me that says to every girl I'm with, "This boy will be different. This boy will take care of you." They all believe it, and so they sleep with me, thinking that soon we'll be married, together, happy.

You can imagine what happens when they learn that I'll do nothing of the sort. I've left girls crying in bed.

I started smoking when I was eleven, and I still do it. I know you do too, and I hate it. But just so that you won't call me a hypocrite, I haven't let you see me smoke for a couple of years now. I drink too, and before we left home, I used to think it was kind of fun to get loaded and drive as fast as I could around town.

Jared put a stop to it.

He said you all needed me too much for that. He told me I was courting Death, and if I didn't watch out, one of these days he'd accept my invitation. Jared always had a knack for putting things clearly, and I sort of wish he were here to tell you what I'm trying to get out. He was good with words. I'm not.

Anyway, I still drink, but I've stopped the driving.

2

I spent maybe half of my freshman year in school. That's a generous estimate. I would go sit by the river or crawl under our porch and think. Sometimes I'd get wasted as early as 10 a.m., and once, when I was broke and out of personal favors, I made the mistake of drinking paint thinner with one of my buddies.

I passed out in Dougie Sherwood's garage that day and didn't make it home until after midnight, the driveway still swimming colorfully as I did so.

I remember how no one was worried. I remember wondering why they worried so much when you were gone but not when I was. I wondered why they trusted me so much, even though I just about put myself in the hospital every day I was missing.

Maybe it was the girl-boy difference that kept them worried for you and not for me. If so they were way off. By age sixteen I'd been laid thirty-two times.

But maybe it was something else.

The implicit assumption seemed to be that I was a good kid and that all the calls about my missing class, all the warnings that I might need to be kept back, all the gentle—and not so gentle—comments from neighbors that maybe I was drinking a little more than I should or fighting a little more than was normal for a boy my age, could all be ignored. Because I was a *good kid*. Because I would *Do right by us*.

At least Jared worried, even if no one else did. He saw more of what I was up to, knew more about what I was doing, and would every once in a while tell me surely and assertively that I was fucking up.

I listened when he told me that, because he didn't do it very often and he didn't do it very loudly. He had a quiet and thoughtful nature. He wasn't prone to rash action like I was. Everything he did was well thought out, part of a plan. So I know he would understand and approve of what I'm about to suggest.

But first let me finish.

3

I got into fights whenever I did go to school. It wasn't because I was getting picked on either. I was the bully. Yes, that's right, at five-five and 112 pounds, a scrappy mess of bones and sinew, I was the bully. And I did it without bodyguards or thug-like cronies either.

I would run at guys for no reason, no reason at all, not even something small, like they bumped into me in the hall. I once pushed Peter Marsh's face into the drinking fountain, just because he happened to be bent over it at the instant I was walking past.

I shot out my arm and shoved his head down. I heard his mouth crunch on the metal, heard him yell out in pain and protest, but I kept walking. I didn't look back. Dougie later told me I had knocked out three of his teeth with that one shove.

Peter never even saw who did it.

The worst fight I was ever in was in eighth grade, right after Dad left. I'd gotten in trouble for a smaller fight with Bradley Rose a couple of days earlier. I had been teasing him for his sissy name, and he swung at me. That was all the invitation I needed to blacken both his eyes.

Anyway, they hauled me into the principal's office for that. I was a puzzle to the principal, Mr. Henderson, and Mr. Diperna, the assistant principal, because up to that time, I had never been caught doing anything. They did a lot of serious talking about how I had to get hold of myself and respect the rights of other people. As Mr. Henderson concluded, with an air of resignation, I had spiraled absolutely out of control, and if I wanted to stay in school, I would have to change my ways and be a good school citizen.

While the two men sat around scratching their heads about me, I wondered how dumb they could be. Dad had left three weeks before the fight, and it didn't take a genius to work out the connection. But they never got around to asking me if anything important had changed in my life that might upset me. The session ended with Mr. Henderson telling me that another fight would mean suspension and that I had to apologize to Bradley.

After school that same day, Mr. Diperna escorted me to the gym, where he had arranged for me to meet Bradley. He and two of his friends were standing in a tight group in front of the locker room.

"Sorry I made fun of you," I said to Bradley, with Mr. Diperna watching.

"Yeah, well, I guess we can forget now," Bradley said.

He didn't exactly accept my apology, but it was good enough for Mr. Diperna.

"You boys shake hands," Mr. Diperna said.

We did as we were told, both of us giving tight smiles.

Mr. Diperna clapped each of us on the shoulder, then turned and walked out of the gym.

4

Bradley waited until Mr. Diperna was out of sight, then he said, "I'm sorry too, Camden. Sorry I fucked your sister last night."

My shoulders stiffened, and I clenched my jaw, but I said nothing. Bradley probably thought that I wasn't crazy enough to risk another fight and that I would keep holding myself back.

"Boy, what a cold bitch! I should have known a girl with a father like that would have a cunt like an ice cube!"

What got me was I could only be half sure he was lying. Even by thirteen, you'd been around, following my example maybe. His words stung me like wasps, and I felt like my brain was on fire.

I rushed at him so fast that he didn't have time to dodge.

I knocked him over and pinned his arms under him. Then I began hitting him in the face. I hit him again and again, watching his head go down and then come back up. Down then back up, like some bizarre jack-in-the-box.

I was dimly aware that people were screaming and yelling at me and trying to catch my fist. I was aware that I had split my fingers on the sharp edges of his broken teeth.

Bradley's face was bloody, and his eyes were showing only whites when someone finally pulled me off of him. I stood up, but before I quit, I ground my boot into his face and mashed in his nose.

He was passed out and couldn't fight back. But I did it anyway. It makes me want to puke remembering it, but at the time it didn't make me sick. At the time, it felt like the only thing to do.

5

Of course I got suspended immediately and kicked

off school grounds. But I never told any of you about it. Jared was the only one who knew. He had to, because we were in the same class. But he forged Mom's signature for me so that I never had to tell anybody.

He didn't like doing that, and the way that he looked at me while he was tracing her name off the blotter of her checkbook was worse punishment than anything the school threw at me.

That was the only time I felt truly ashamed for something I had done.

I don't remember much about what I did during those days that I wasn't able to go to school. Sometimes I got drunk and hung out down by the creek. Sometimes I just wandered around town or took long walks to nowhere.

But all the time I kept thinking of what Bradley had said, and I wondered and wondered if it was true. I didn't think so, but I couldn't be sure. And not knowing almost killed me.

Almost killed Bradley Rose too.

His nose was broken, and he lost four teeth. I'd crunched in parts of his skull and broken his jaw, all in addition to the two black eyes I had already given him. They treated him for head trauma in the ER at the hospital. I heard later that he had to have reconstructive surgery on his nose just to breathe normally.

I never saw him again. He had transferred to a school on the other side of town, by the time my suspension ended and I was allowed back. Word was that he was too scared to come anywhere near me.

This gave me no pleasure, the way it did Dougie and Richie and some others. Instead of the fearful admiration of my classmates, I kept seeing the way Jared looked at me when he was bent over the checkbook.

6

I wondered then, and continued to wonder, how it was that I was still the *good kid*? I wondered how none of you could see what your good kid was doing: sending obnoxious but harmless boys to the plastic surgeons in Jacksonville; drinking himself unconscious on moonshine; screwing around with too many girls and leaving them as quickly as he found them; ignoring his own older brother's love, which he gave with a remarkable and quiet patience.

I wondered then, and I wonder now, why none of you ever saw who the good kid really was. Why did everyone always look to me?

Jared is the reason I'm even alive today. He's the one who kept me from going out in a blaze of fury and maybe taking out somebody else as well. He's the one who said, finally, when we were around fifteen, "Will, it's one thing to kill yourself. It's another thing to kill a whole family."

He was talking metaphorically, I think.

Talking about killing our *chances*, but at the time, I jumped, because lately I had been thinking of suicide in a new way. I saw it as the only way I

116

could escape from your unconditional love and approval. It was the only thing I could do to stop the family from depending on me, even if it didn't stop you from loving me.

That love carried so much responsibility that it scared the shit out of me. I didn't want it. I did everything possible to push it away. And yet you all persisted. It was Jared who made me see that day that nothing I ever did would send your love away. He's the one who taught me to accept it and, eventually, to embrace it.

He told me this with grave resignation, and I realized as suddenly as I realized the truth of what he was saying that he had been trying to win that sort of love and approval for himself for as long as I had tried to be rid of it.

He came to understand that he could not take the burden on himself, any more than I could shake it off. It was not ours to give or take. It was something bestowed or withheld that we could not change, only acknowledge.

I'd just turned fifteen, and I understood that the responsibility was mine for life, however long that was. I began to believe that cutting off my life with the pistol I'd bought would not be anything but selfish. If I took my life, I also took the lives of all those who loved me. And that was getting to be a hell of a lot of people.

Slowly, my fights stopped. Slowly, I went to school more than a bare majority of the time. Slowly, I stopped seeking out the girls, even though they never stopped seeking me.

Jared saved me from going down a very dark road.

Not just for selfless reasons, and not just because he loved me so much—although we did love one another and shared the special connection that only brothers close in age will ever know or understand. Jared gave me my life. And that's why I felt it only fitting that I should give him his.

7

I'm sure you've already figured this out, but I knew Jared was leaving. We decided together, in an unspoken agreement, that one of us should go. This was about the time we saw that Mom was really losing it. About when she was talking about taking after Dad, but before she'd actually done anything. It was about the time of that horrible thing with Benjy Magee and soon after you came to me in the middle of the night and said you wanted to kill yourself. You didn't know I'd been thinking the same thing less than a year before.

I saw that our life was killing you, not like a bullet would, with one swift explosion, but like starving, long and drawn out. If you leave a picture under dripping water for a long time, the colors all wear away. The picture becomes blurred, faceless. Finally, the image disappears entirely.

Finally it disappears entirely.

I felt like that was what was happening to anyone who stayed with this family. We were fading away, forming one indistinct mass of hurt, and soon there would be nothing left for us, nothing left of us except for the pain that we all shared.

I wanted something better for at least one of us. And I knew that the one of us who deserved better, who needed better, was Jared. We pretended to play Rock paper scissors to decide who would leave, but I knew that no matter how the game turned out, he was going to have to leave. I couldn't let him stay here. It would have killed him.

So he left. I made him go.

I did it to save the brother who had unobtrusively saved his whole family. For the brother who was always so good, but never got any reward. I wanted him to be recognized somewhere out there in the world. I thought, when he left, that I could stop the fading. That I could turn the handle of that faucet and save what was left of us all.

That I could curb the effects of time.

Instead, time found us all crouching in the pickup. It found you stealing out at night like a criminal and sharing yourself with stupid, undeserving boys.

It found me waiting up all night and sneaking a smoke outside the door, crying for Jared, and wishing there were something I could do to save you all.

It found Jen silent and watchful, Sarah mistrustful, even of us. It found Tommy finally able to say *Daddy*, but never able to put a face to the word.

We were even more faded than we had been, and nothing I could try would stop the process. I knew

I had to do something to keep us whole, to keep us *real*. And that's when I came up with what I'm about to tell you.

8

I've told you all this, all this random stuff, for a couple of reasons. First, I wanted to make clear to you that I am not perfect, I never was, and that what I'm doing is not a last-ditch effort to secure myself a position as a saint.

Second, I wanted you to know that it's not as though this is a rash decision on my part. I admit that I've made a lot of those, but this one is for real.

I thought about it all the times I waited up for you and even after you were back asleep. I thought it through a million different times in a million different ways, and this is what I kept coming back to. I think it's the only solution.

I've decided to kill myself.

Casey 2002

"I've decided to kill myself."

I hear Will say it, but it doesn't have any meaning at first.

I've just come back from spending a couple of hours with a guy named Jacob. Right now we're in Missouri, not too far outside of Kansas City. It's about as far north as we've ever gone, and already I feel people marveling at our accents. We're tenting tonight, out here in the middle of someone's field. It's spring again, though cool and wet, and the flowers are starting to bloom.

Jacob showed me where there's a strawberry patch. They aren't ripe enough to eat yet, he says, but soon they will be. Then he and I can go pick them.

I look at the tiny yellow berries and the unreal white flowers that surround them, then at his open and trusting face. I cannot take any pleasure in bringing the truth to him. So I smile quietly and say that I would love that.

He smiles back and takes my hand. I feel that his hands are rough with calluses and see that the nails are cut short to keep them clean, but a small half-moon of dirt has snuck in anyway. I raise his hands to my mouth and kiss them softly. They smell of pine tar and Ivory soap. It smells wonderful.

I lie back and watch the stars with him. He points out the constellations he can recognize, and I admire them as though I have never heard of them before. I enjoy myself more than I have in a long time.

That is what is real. The strawberry patch and the smell of Jacob's hands. Those things are real. Not this.

It just can't be.

2

When I return to our tents, Will is waiting up for me as usual. But as I approach, leaving Jacob with a quick kiss, I see something glowing in Will's hand. Sarcastic comments race to mind, because Will and I fought only this morning about my cigarettes. But the comments all die in mid-thought as I glimpse his face.

My first guess is that someone is hurt, someone has died. Somewhere something has gone horribly wrong.

I sprint now, moving closer and closer to the tents, but realize as I approach that he is the only one awake. I listen cautiously and count the rhythmic breathing of four other people.

Then I freeze about five feet from Will, trying to understand what is going on. He doesn't get up to greet me as he usually does, not even to sigh heavily. He is staring straight at me, but I don't think he can actually see me. His eyes are glazed over, and for a second I wonder if he's smoking a joint.

Then he does look at me, and immediately I wish he hadn't.

His eyes don't look like him. The phrase *animal eyes* flashes absurdly through my mind because I can't imagine that intensity, that feverish panic, in a person.

Yet those eyes are in my brother's face. His beautiful, delicately featured face. His hair flops into it. We haven't cut his hair in what is getting to be a very long time. It rests on his forehead, curling softly in the humidity. Despite the eyes, it is my brother's face, and when he speaks it is my brother's voice I hear.

"Casey, can we talk for a minute?"

I nod, afraid that if I open my mouth, I will spill out a flood of questions and worries, especially ones about those eyes that are not my brother's. He gets up and throws the cigarette to the ground, crushing it with a bare foot.

I wince. He doesn't.

He begins to wander back the way I have come. I follow at a slight distance, and when he turns, I freeze as though we are playing Red Light Green Light.

He comes back towards me.

"Why are you scared?" he asks gently.

I'm not sure what to say to him. I don't think I can tell him that I'm scared of him. It sounds ridiculous to me and would sound even more so to him. He's my older brother, for God's sake. He's never done anything to hurt me. He's done everything, always, to help me. He's held me at night. He's even risked his own life for me before.

So why am I frightened of him now?

As he takes my hand and leads me even farther from the tents, I realize suddenly that I am not frightened *of* him, but frightened *for* him. There is a fervent resolve in his eyes that I have seen only once before—on the night that Jared left.

As I stare into his face at those eyes, it comes back to me in a flood of memory. I am entirely enveloped.

3

Jen and I had been lying awake.

I think even Sarah might have been up. We had all felt the vague sense of unease enfolding our house for the past few days, the way you can tell when a big storm is about to hit. So when we heard the springs in the boys' room shriek not once, but twice, we knew that whatever it was, it was happening.

We sneaked downstairs into the kitchen. There we saw Will, holding Tommy and facing Jared. Jared had one foot out the screen door and one foot still in the kitchen. He gripped a paper bag under one arm and was looking back desperately, fearfully, as though he wanted nothing so much as for someone to stop him.

Perhaps that is why no one did.

Jared and Will had locked gazes, and as I clutched

at Will, maybe trying to make sure that he didn't leave, maybe just overcome by panic, I saw the expression in his eyes. Jared saw it too, and with one last, longing glance at all of us, he let the screen door click shut and padded softly across the porch.

We stayed still.

I heard his shoes crunch in the gravel of our driveway. And then I heard no more. He was gone. The look had faded from Will's eyes. It was as though he knew that he had made the sacrifice irrevocably, and that now that there was no turning back, he could accept it.

I shiver as I recall this. His eyes tell the same story now. He is going to make some kind of sacrifice for all of us. Suddenly I understand Jared's fear. I do not want to be in on this. I do not want to know what it is.

4

I wish desperately for us to be in the strawberry patch.

We stop about fifteen feet away from it and sit down under a sycamore tree at the edge of the field. He offers me a cigarette, and this scares me even more. I refuse. He looks thoughtful, then lights one for himself.

"Casey, I have a lot to say," he begins. "Can you let me get it all out at once? It'll be a lot easier without any interruption. Will you do that for me?"

"Yes," is all I say.

I don't think I could interrupt even if I wanted to. I'm too panic-stricken. All I want is to run away from Will and whatever it is that he has to tell me without interruption.

I want to run back to Jacob and his callused-but-gentle hands. I find that I am unable to move, so running becomes out of the question. Will is studying my face. I wonder if my eyes look like animal eyes too.

"Okay." He drags deeply on what is left of the cigarette before crushing it into the grass. Then he pulls his knees up to his chest and hugs them, staring at the sky and looking very young.

He begins. "I am far from perfect."

From here, he makes a speech that retraces some things I'd rather forget, some hurtful things from our past, but they are not the worst part. The worst part is not remembering the incident with Benjy Magee and how I thought my life was over until Will shot off that pistol.

It's not the memory of Will stumbling in after school reeking of rye whiskey and sometimes of vomit. It's not the thought of his cuts and bruises and broken bones or the rumors I would always hear about the injuries he gave other boys.

The worst part is that I know where all the remembering is headed. I knew even before he began, knew from the look I saw in his animal eyes.

My heart starts pounding double-time, and I want to thrust my fingers in my ears before he gets to the end. All the words his voice is narrating, pronouncing carefully in his familiar, gentle voice, are just a prelude to that last horrible thing.

I'm caught in the tunnel of his speech, being forced to one sure, unalterable conclusion. I am helpless to stop it. I dread it. I try not to hear it. But it is no use. He ends with it anyway.

"I've decided to kill myself."

5

At first this has no meaning, because I cannot let it. I cannot let the sickening emotions I've been feeling attach themselves to those words, because if I do, it will infuse the words with the power of reality. I battle myself, trying to divest the statement of any meaning. I try to make it a string of five nonsense words.

Banana-fanna-me-mi-mo-manna.

Suicide.

The word forces its way into my consciousness, despite my efforts. The word makes it real. The strawberry patch is moving farther and farther away from me. My older brother wants to commit suicide.

I cry out. I don't know if it's anything articulate. And then I shout, "No!!"

I know I've said that. After that it's a blur. I think Will is holding me. As he does, some other face swims momentarily in front of his. Incoherently, I wonder if he is already dead and that is why I am so hysterical. Perhaps it is really Mom who is holding me. Or Dad.

But then Will's face is back, and his voice is back, and I let him hold me in his thin arms.

Will 2002

I'm telling Casey all of this and watching her face to see how she's taking it.

Her eyes look funny, and she's not acting at all like herself. My Casey would have snapped at me about smoking, would have interrupted me throughout what I'm saying, and certainly wouldn't have eyes dancing with fear.

I fight the urge a couple of times to ask her if she's even hearing what I'm saying. She looks so far away.

I finish, and I can tell she has heard.

Her face changes, convulses almost. At first she says nothing. She sits there, legs tucked up under her, hair hanging in her face, partially masking her contorted expression.

I wish she'd say something. The silence is heavy, almost poisonous. I feel like I'm sucking it in with the thick air around me and that it's weakening my resolve.

My heart is knocking so hard in my chest that I feel like it might crack a rib. I'm scared as hell, and she probably knows it. I'm sure it's written in my face. I told her this not just because someone in the family has to know what's going on, but because I needed someone to help me along, to reassure me, to convince me to go through with it.

I do not need this silence.

She cries out so suddenly that I actually spring back. Rather than bringing comfort, her hoarse cry terrifies me. It doesn't sound like her, doesn't even sound human.

She meets my eyes then and screams again, but this time I hear what she is saying: "No!!"

She falls to the ground, moaning into the grass, and cries. Her sobs seem to come from deep inside. They shake her entire body. I scoop her up and am amazed at how light she is, how small she feels in my arms.

She thrashes against me, and my surprise at her weight is replaced by surprise at her strength. Her thin arms are nothing but muscle, and they attempt to wrench mine apart.

We struggle together until she looks right into my face and calms. I hold her close and rub her back for the better part of an hour, humming under my breath just like Dad used to when we were sick. She relaxes.

Finally she pulls back and looks at me.

2

"You can't mean that."

I look at her carefully, trying to judge whether or not she is calm enough to hear the reasons I have prepared. She lights up a cigarette. I take this as a good sign and decide to press on with this. I'd better. It's going to get light before too long.

"I do."

She drags deeply on the cigarette and stares at me for a long moment before speaking again.

"No. You don't. You're just ... just confused. Will, I know that you want to help us, but what makes you think that leaving us all alone would do that? Dad's gone. Jared is gone. You can't leave too. That will kill Mom. It will kill *all* of us."

'And besides," she speaks more quickly now as though some irrefutable argument has just occurred to her. "You said that Jared stopped you before. You said he *saved* your *life*. Why would you now take away the life he gave you? It's not fair to him, is it?"

It's just what I was expecting, and I'm glad because now I don't feel so unsure of myself. Already I feel my resolve growing, and I clutch at whatever I can to preserve it. Before the night is out, I will need all the help I can get.

"Jared gave me my life, and I was glad. I was glad because it meant that I could use it to help him. To help you, all of you. If I had done it back when I was fifteen, if I had died, it would have been the end of everything. It would have destroyed you all because you refused to rely on Jared. You refused to have anyone but me be strong for you. So if I was weak it would have been the end."

"And it won't *now*? What's so different about now? Will, we still need you! We still depend on you, especially Mom! Jared isn't here. We *still* need you to be strong for us."

"I *am* being strong for you!"

I feel my voice getting louder and make an effort to keep it under control. The last thing I want is for Casey to think I am angry, or worse, that I'm crazy, or anything except logical.

"Can't you see that?" I ask. "What is strength except doing what will help those you care about, no matter what the risk to you? What is bravery if not trading your life for the lives of those ... those you ... love?"

3

My voice slows and breaks on the last word, and I am angry and disgusted to find that I am crying. This will not help to convince her of the coolly logical, well-thought-out decision I was hoping to convey. I continue anyway, because now that I have started, I need to get it all out, no matter what the cost.

"And what good would it be if I used the life I almost threw away—my life, that I didn't care about for so long—for no one except myself? I didn't go on living for me. I did it for you. I did it for all of you. And now ... now I see that living for you is not helping. I haven't turned the water off. We're all still fading, so fast that it scares me. Have you talked to Jen recently? Have any of us? It's not because she's stupid. She's smart, Casey, too damn smart to lead this kind of life. She's just so hurt and *disgusted* by all of this that she can't stand to talk anymore. She's so fucking disgusted. She's *wasted*, Casey. This life

136

is eating her away just like ... just like it has you
... ."

I can't go on. I'm really crying now. I rub furiously at my eyes with balled-up fists, but it's no good. I tip my head back and let the tears run down my cheeks as I finish shakily.

"And the little ones," I say. "What about them? How long can this go on for them? If they live like this, they'll never know a home, or a family. Because this doesn't feel like a family. The lines on the picture have faded that far already. It's all blurry. A blur of pain and misery. But if you look closely enough, you can still pick out individual shapes. And that's why I want to stop us fading. I want to stop while that's still possible, before you all collapse together. You have to be *real* people. You can't let this consume you. It got you, Casey, and it was the most ... I couldn't stand ... ."

The tears come again, but it's okay this time. I've said almost everything I wanted. I give up and fall to the ground, pressing my face into the dewy grass. I don't wipe the tears this time, but I feel a light touch against my exposed cheek and realize that Casey is doing it for me. I sit up, and she holds me as I cry, the way I held her before.

4

We stay that way a long time, and as we do, I feel a sense of calm assurance growing within me. It already feels as though she is taking on what I am losing; that I am bestowing something upon her. I smooth her hair back. She does the same to mine. We both give watery smiles. Then she takes my hand softly.

"Will, let it be me."

I had expected this as well, but find it strangely difficult to give my explanation for why it cannot be her, why it must be me. I shake my head.

"That wouldn't be enough."

"Why not?"

"It wouldn't be ... shocking ... enough to get her to stop."

I try to choose my words carefully, but her face has puckered. I hope she is not interpreting this to mean that I think Mom doesn't care about her life.

I rush on.

"Of course she would be devastated, but you ... you already have a rebellion thing going. Mom knows you leave at night, and she knows what you do ... ."

I stop at the funny expression on her face. She smiles at me, a real smile that I recognize from the days when we were very young, a smile of hazy memory.

"You know what I did tonight? I talked about strawberries and held hands under the stars."

"Nothing more?"

"No."

"Is it always nothing more?"

"No. Sometimes it's everything. Or nothing. Tonight felt like everything I ever wanted. I ... I liked it better than the sex stuff."

"I never had times like that. I'm so glad you do."

"Me too."

Her smile is still there, and an answering one stretches across my face. Then I feel a leaden weight in my stomach. I had forgotten why we were talking. The first gray light of dawn reminds me. I shove on, although it would be so much easier to talk through till day and let the whole thing pass without incident. I think of Jen and the kids.

I know I can't do that.

5

"Still, Casey, Mom doesn't know that. She's already sort of written you off. She thinks you're a lost cause. It has to be me. That's the only thing that would be shocking enough. It's the only wake-up call we can give her. Believe me." I laugh, even though nothing is funny. "I wouldn't suggest it if it weren't the only thing I could think of. It has to be me, and it has to be now."

I pull the pistol out of my pocket and lay it on the ground between us. She stares at it with curiosity and revulsion. Then she picks it up, and wildly I worry that she is about to put it to her own temple.

I relax as I remember that the bullets are safe in my other pocket. She holds it, testing its weight, and looks into my eyes. Without dropping her gaze, she places it back on the ground and nods.

"Yes. It has to be you."

Her voice is cool, but there is moisture gathering in her eyes again, making them glossy. She throws her arms around me and nearly knocks me to the ground.

"But not now! Please, Will, not now! Not now not now not now not now ... ."

She is chanting it again and again like a spell to keep dark magic at bay. I don't want to do it now either, but I know that I must act quickly or I will lose my nerve. I shush her quiet, but this time she doesn't leave my arms.

"Now, Case. I have to."

She says nothing, so I say the final thing I feel is necessary.

"Case, I also think, I'm not positive, but I think, that when Jared hears about this, he will come home."

Now she is surprised and pulls back to look into my face again. She still says nothing, but her eyes ask me to continue.

"Jared was always the one who thought things through. If he sees this as rash, like always, he'll step in to save you from me. If he sees it as thoughtful, he'll know why I did it and do his best to help with what I intended."

I fall silent for a moment, and so does she.

Then she whispers, "You really miss him, don't you? It killed you to let him go."

The last is not a question, but a statement.

"I would dream about him coming home and wake up crying," I say. "Sometimes when I'd hear the screen door click shut, I'd think it was him. I think he'll come back now. But if he doesn't, or maybe even if he does, you're going to have to be ... like me. I know you can. You just were. You're strong. You're brave. I know you can do this."

She's shaking her head and not even trying to stop the tears flowing from her eyes, but I know she will do it when I am gone. I nod at her, and slowly, she nods back. I embrace her again, and although neither of us speaks, we know we are saying goodbye.

6

I am the one who pulls away. I'm dimly aware that I must be crying too, but now it doesn't seem to matter. My resolve is the strongest it has ever been, and the light over the field is growing brighter. I must act quickly.

"Casey, go back to the tent. Lie there. Do not come out when you hear the shot. Do not wake anyone. Let them wake on their own. But go now, Case, so that I can do this before my courage breaks."

She is nodding all the while and backing away from me, but she never takes her eyes from my face.

I load the gun while she is still watching, but this is too much for her. She runs at me and nearly knocks me to the ground. She would have if I hadn't anticipated it.

I fight her off. It is surprisingly difficult, even more of a struggle than before. She thrashes and claws desperately. I finally manage to push her away.

I see that I have scratched her across one cheek and that it is bleeding. I move closer and kiss the spot. She is calm now.

"Goodbye, Casey. I'm doing this because I love you."

She speaks too although her voice is choked. "I love you too, Will. And you're wrong. You are perfect." She kisses my cheek then and turns and runs to the tent as though something frightful were chasing her.

I sit beneath the tree again, staring at the tents for a full fifteen minutes to make sure that she is not coming out and has not awakened anyone else. I see that the sky is wavering on the verge of full-blown pink.

As I click off the safety of the gun everything seems remarkably clear. I can see each individual blade of grass and the morning dew condensing on them. I can see the silhouette of the tree branches above me and the waving corn in the distance.

I see the tents, know that they contain my family, and in my mind an endless series of images plays. I am doing this for my family, and in the end it will be best.

Confident in this, I place the barrel of the gun inside my mouth, aim upward, and tighten my finger on the trigger.

Casey 2003

We are back home now.

It's the weirdest feeling I've ever had.

I can remember when we first left and spent all that time driving on back roads and sleeping in unfamiliar beds. I thought then that nothing could feel stranger than waking up and not knowing where I was. Now the strangest thing I can imagine is waking up at home.

We didn't get here right away.

First we went to Grandma's house and stayed there while Mom recovered—if you can call it that. What Will did happened back in June, but it took her until about September to be able to speak again.

I'm the one who drove us home after the funeral. If it had been possible, I mean not so expensive, I would have had Will buried back here. I hate that he's in some tiny cemetery in Eminence, Missouri, where no one knows or cares who he is or why he died.

I practically had to bribe them to bury him there. In the Bible Belt, they aren't too sympathetic about suicides. If he had been one of their own people, they would have been nicer. I know small towns well enough to know that.

The night Will died was horrible. I wish it would come back only in snatches, like the months when Mom wouldn't talk or eat, but it plays in my mind larger than life and twice as vivid.

I ran back to the tent when he told me to, and I didn't bother being quiet. As I threw myself down on my sleeping bag, I noticed vaguely that Jen was also awake and sitting up. I wondered how much she knew. I sat up and looked at her, trying to figure out if she had guessed.

She was crying. She had.

She spoke quietly to me, although whenever she spoke it was always quiet. She said, "I saw him take the gun."

I looked at her and realized that, despite her blond hair and blue eyes, she looked much like I used to. It was her frightened expression that triggered it, I think.

She held out her hand to me, and I saw that it was shaking. I grasped it in both of mine. With a sudden sob she climbed into my sleeping bag with me, and we sat there, clutching each other.

"Jen? Case?" The voice was very small, but not at all sleepy.

Sarah was sitting up in bed.

I was sure she'd been awake as long as Jen had. It was just like the night that Jared left. We had all felt it. I had felt it as I left with Jacob. It was not the normal tension that accompanied my dates, not older-brother anger or protective instinct. I wrote it off, but the special tension was the reason I knew, before he told me, what Will was going to do.

Sarah climbed quickly over to us and knelt down.

We each grabbed her hands as well, sitting together in a circle, keeping a vigil. We bowed our heads as though praying, and for all I know they were. I wasn't. I was concentrating all my energy on not hearing the gunshot, but part of me still wanted just to have it over with.

My eyes were screwed up tightly so that flashing patterns danced against a black background, and I was squeezing Jen and Sarah for all I was worth.

But still no shot came.

"Why is it taking so goddamn long?" asked Jen suddenly, her voice harsh and raw and louder than it had been in years.

We raised our heads so that we were all looking at one another and at that instant, like some sort of terrible magic, a single shot shattered the silence.

3

I expected something to rip inside me, I expected to go into hysterics. But I did not.

It was Jen who broke down, Sarah who followed, and me who stood by to pick up the pieces. I felt then that the torch had been passed, as Will probably knew it had been before he said goodbye.

I sat there holding my two sisters for what felt like hours. Maybe it even was. Mom was so exhausted that she didn't even wake up at the gunshot.

What finally broke us apart was Tommy standing in the tent opening, thumb in mouth, green eyes wide, blond curls hanging into his face. We'd been trying to get him to stop his thumb-sucking, and for a minute he pulled out his thumb, as if expecting to be scolded. Then after sensing something was wrong with his sisters, he returned his thumb to his mouth,

The other two girls pulled away from me, and we all buried our faces in our hands. We rubbed at the tears that coursed down our cheeks.

Sarah was the first to speak, her voice rough with sobbing.

"Mom's going to ask why we didn't wake her up."

This was true.

Sarah was absentmindedly braiding her waist-length red hair into a long plait. Where the color came from was a family mystery. Will said, only half-joking, that maybe she had a different father. Mom was quick to say that Sarah was actually the spitting image of her mother as a girl. That was something none of us could disprove.

I had taken Tommy into my lap, and he was cuddling against me, unaware of what exactly was wrong, but knowing that something was. The mood was heavy, but almost serene.

Then Jen said, "Fuck her."

Her words were loud and abrupt in the quiet of the tent. I had never heard Jen swear like that before, even though by her age, I had cursed out

Mom and Jared and Will with the vocabulary of a hardened criminal. Even Sarah had been known to swear more than Jen.

We all focused on her, more stunned by the ferocity behind her words than by the words themselves.

She wasn't looking at us.

She was staring off at the side of the tent where you could see the branches of the big sycamore—the sycamore beneath which Will lay dead—waving in silhouette. Her knees were hugged up to her already ample chest, and several feet of a bare leg showed from beneath her nightshirt, but she looked far from sexy. Her voice was quiet, and somehow that made the anger more serious, more real.

"It's her fault anyway," Jen said. "All of this is her fault. We wouldn't be in this goddamn field, we wouldn't have missed years and years of school, we wouldn't always be angry. We might be able to be proud, and our older brother sure as *hell* wouldn't be lying *dead* five yards from where we're sitting, if she hadn't been so fucking *crazy* as to take off after Dad!!"

Jen's voice had been rising as she spoke, until by the end she was yelling, with tears squeezing their way out of her fierce eyes, spit flying from the corners of her mouth, her cheeks blazing with the effort of holding everything in for so long. Yet she was still not looking at us. She continued, halting after every couple of words to try to stay composed enough to talk, succeeding only partially.

"It's *because* she's so goddamn crazy that she fucked us all over too! I hate her! I'm not kidding, I fucking *hate* her!"

Jen directed the last at us, as though we had been accusing her of lying, which, seeing her that way, none of us had. Then she turned toward us, and her rage seemed to ebb at the sight of our faces.

She broke down, sobbing, but she pulled away as I stretched out my hand to hold her. She spluttered something which I could barely make out before she truly broke into sobs.

"I just wish that it hadn't happened."

Nobody asked her whether she meant Dad leaving or Mom taking us to chase him, Jared's departure or Will's suicide. Or any of the years and years that had lain in between.

We all knew that she meant all of it. We knew because we wished it too. Sarah reached over to hold her, and this time she did not pull away. I was still clutching Tommy to me. Neither of us was crying. I think we were both overwhelmed.

Sarah wasn't crying either, but she was looking at Jen with a face full of pride and anger and what was so unmistakably a fierce love that I suddenly wished I hadn't seen the look.

I could tell from her face that she was upset even more for Jen than for herself. It reminded me so much of the way I felt about Will that it was almost unbearable.

Eventually, Jen's sobs quieted. She rubbed her eyes with the palms of her hands, and then fell silent.

"But we do have to tell her," Sarah said. "Now. Before she finds him herself."

Sarah had brought up something else that I had been dreading. I knew Will was dead. I knew he had shot himself. But I did not think I could stand to find his body. I could not stand to see something that looked so much like my brother, but was not. But the alternative, I realized, was to let Mom find him, and I knew instinctively that Will's plan had not involved that.

I put Tommy down, and left the tent without a word.

4

I stood in the dewy morning light.

The sun was shining brightly, and the day was fair. It was still somewhat early, probably around six or seven, and nothing was moving yet in the farmland around us.

I took in the scene, keeping my eyes as far away from the tree as I possibly could. But they fell there eventually. They had to.

It was too far away to see much, but I saw a flash of his blue shirt and the stains on it. I tried to halt my eyes before they raised themselves to his head, but they went anyway. They fixed on a bloody mess entangled with his dark hair.

I moved closer and felt as though it were not my own free will driving me. The scene slid into preternaturally sharp focus, as if I had put on a pair of special glasses.

From the neck down there was not much different about Will except for the bloodstains on his shirt, which were oh so familiar from those dozens of schoolyard fights.

Please god please god please god I wish he just had a bloody nose. Oh please we dreamed it, we all hallucinated together, and he's just cut himself, and just like all the other times, he'll start awake and grin and say, Gee I'm a mess. Case can you help me clean this up.

His hand was resting limply on his chest, and the gun had slid out of his grasp to fall between his legs.

He's just dozing and he'll pick up the gun and laugh and say he wanted to keep me safe, just like that time with Benjy Magee, and he'll always be there for me to help me and protect me, and he didn't buy the gun to shoot himself, back when he was fifteen and wanted to and he didn't end up using it for that anyway, because he's not dead, he's just asleep, and the gun slipped out of his hand.

But above his neck there was no question.

He was dead. His face and head were unrecognizable, barely held together by the remaining bone and muscle. His eyes were wide and staring and still a beautiful brown, but not the way they had been before. They were a pretty color, but they were not alive. They were not Will.

I didn't look carefully, but I could tell the back of his skull had been blown out. His normally dark hair was even darker in what looked to me like a gallon of blood. Rivulets had trickled down the sides of his cheeks like tears. More had come from inside his mouth and spilled down his shirt, the way vomit had often done back when he drank too much. That was where the stains had come from.

His head lolled unnaturally against the tree. The

flaky, silvery trunk of the sycamore was spattered with bright crimson and with other more solid-looking pieces of my brother.

I was frozen in place, trembling, but still not crying.

Not fully aware of what I was doing, I reached down and took the gun from him. I could see more blood on it, and knew that it must be all over my hands, but I did not care. I could tell that it was still loaded and briefly considered shooting myself.

But I let that pass as easily as if I had considered trying to fly. It was not the plan. Instead, I turned on my heel like a soldier in drill practice and walked slowly back toward Mom's pup tent. I saw the other three standing by our tent and watching me in terrible fascination.

I almost told them not to go near Will, but I knew they wouldn't. That had been my job, and I had done it. I realized they were following me to tell Mom.

For some reason we were walking single-file, even though I felt like clutching them all to me. We walked in age order too, Tommy trotting at the rear, attempting to keep up with our longer strides. As I stopped in front of the tent, I drew in a deep breath as though I were diving into a lake. Then I pushed aside the flap.

5

I saw my mother sprawled out on the ground, and as I looked at her, I felt that I couldn't do this. The anger that I had summoned on Will's behalf, on Jen's, on all of our's, melted into the air.

She was sleeping quietly and heavily. Her hair was not as long as it used to be, but still reached her shoulders. It was brown with some natural strawberry-blond highlights. A strand lay over her cheek, and I wanted to reach down and push it off her face, until I remembered the blood that still covered my hands.

My mother looked younger than Sarah, younger than Tommy even. And as I watched her it came to me that she acted that way too, that she had ever since Dad left. His leaving had broken something in her that years of hardship had not, and she had seen no other choice but to pursue him, however difficult or illogical that might be. She pursued him for the most childish reason possible—she needed him, was helpless without him, despite the men and the money and us.

My musings were interrupted as she stirred awake and her eyes lit on me. She blinked confusedly and sat up, still in the daze of sleep. Then I slid into sharper focus for her, and she got a better look at me, at the gun, the blood on my hands, my dirt-and-tear-streaked face. Her mouth opened and her face formed a question.

I answered it before she spoke.

"Mom, it's Will. Will is dead."

Her face crumpled, and I thought it was to cry, so I stepped forward toward her. As I bent down, she sprang up quickly and slapped me hard across the face.

I fell over more from surprise than anything. She did not give me time to regain myself, but dove on me and began hitting and punching me. I wondered desperately where the gun had gone and worried that she might use it on me.

I was utterly baffled about what was going on until she began shrieking at me.

"You *bitch*! You heartless bitch! It's not enough that you hurt me every day! Not enough that you set a bad example for your sisters! Now you had to take away my boy! He was the *only* one I had left! He was *all* I had left! How *could* you do that to your own *brother*?"

I scuttled back out of the tent, almost tripping over the gun. I was fending her off as best I could and trying to explain as I did so.

"Mom, no! Will killed *himself*! I didn't do anything! He did it *himself*!"

But she wasn't listening. She clawed at my face and hit me with her shoulder, knocking the wind out of me. She kept coming at me, and I wondered if she actually meant to kill me.

I managed to regain my feet, and as she was about to tackle me again, the gun went off. Mom froze, and I turned to see Sarah, her hair loosened from its plait and wild around her face. Her features were contorted in anger and fear.

She was pointing the gun at Mom.

Flashes of the incident with Benjy Magee made the situation even more terrible than it would otherwise have been. I realized she hadn't aimed the shot at us, but it was clear also that she *could*. I wondered, just as I had with Will, where and how she had picked up the skill. I guessed what turned out to be correct—Will had taught her. Could he possibly have seen something like this coming?

The gun trembled in Sarah's small hands, but her expression did not waver, and when she spoke her voice didn't either.

Mom gulped some deep breaths and sat down hard on the ground. I ran back to where the others were standing, then turned to face her. Jen took my hand and squeezed it, blood now also covering hers.

Sarah lowered the gun and spoke.

"He did it himself, Mom. You could go look, but I don't think you want to."

We all looked toward the tree where Will lay. Mom gave one enormous shudder, and then collapsed on the ground. From that moment, she became meeker than a small child and did not say a word to anyone.

6

I arranged everything, the burial, the trip home, everything.

Mom did not speak to anyone, although she allowed herself to be led around like a toddler. For a while she wouldn't eat, but eventually she began again.

I don't think she ever meant to die. I don't think she ever missed Will as much as I did either. Perhaps I'm wrong, not giving her enough credit for how much she loved her own son, but I don't think so. I don't think she loved Will the way I did, as himself, but that she loved him as a substitute for Dad. After all, they looked alike, and he cared for us better than Dad had ever done, so why not just love him as Dad when the real thing wasn't there?

Sometimes during that summer, the longest one of my life, I despised my mother for how upset she was. I felt that she had not earned the right to be as devastated by Will's death as she was. If anyone deserved to be catatonic, I did.

Will was the only boy I had ever loved. I did not love my father even when he was around. I knew he was a sad man, and I knew that he loved us, but I just couldn't love him. He was the reason I would fall asleep to Mom's crying. He was the reason I was always hungry.

And, above all, he was the reason my brother Will came home from school with black eyes and bloody noses, even before the *real* fights started. I could not love someone who caused that.

I should have loved Jared, but I never did.

I could see, anyone could see, that Will loved him with an almost frightening intensity. I think maybe that's why I never could. He already had Will, and I felt like that should be enough for anybody. Besides, Jared's quiet presence did nothing to reassure or protect me. I would much rather have had Will punching my schoolyard tormentors and then holding me quietly when we were alone.

Maybe I was also jealous of the unquestioning and unconditional way in which Jared and Will supported each other. They would fight, sure, but I always felt like it was more for show than anything.

Will knew Jared was right. Jared knew he was right. All that remained was for Will to admit it, which never took that long. There was never any question, never any hard feelings.

I always hated it that Jared knew better than Will.

I should also love Tommy, but, although I want to keep him safe, I find myself unable to work up the feeling. He arrived on the scene too late. The damage to our family had already been done by then.

I felt as though my heart had taken so many hits that it just wouldn't work anymore. It wasn't broken, but it was bruised so many times over that it had simply gone numb. I couldn't let myself love anyone new.

And the only person I already loved was Will.

7

Some would say that I should have loved the boys I slept with. There were not as many as everyone in the family thinks. There were some, but they were my decision.

It is simply not true that all boys are looking for sex all the time. Some of them are, but most of the time I wouldn't even detect it. I've met so many boys who considered themselves hopelessly in love with me that I cannot believe men do not crave love and commitment as much as women do, even if they hide it better.

I used to take a dark pleasure in letting those boys know that I did not love them and never would. I wanted them to feel as deadened as I did, and I did my best to bring it about.

But after a couple of years, after Paul really, the whole process lost much of its appeal. I realized that I did not know those boys as I thought I did and that it was unfair of me to want to make their lives worse. How did I know that their lives weren't bad enough already? So instead, I was neutral, neither cold and distant nor warm and welcoming. I discovered that this actually made me feel better, less angry at least, than I had before.

It was an improvement, but I still didn't love them.

Will was the only boy I loved. He was the only one who knew how I thought and understood how I felt. He was also the only one I would listen to. He is the only reason, really, that I never took a leaf from Dad's book and left my family. He is the only reason that I am still here at all, in more ways than one.

8

It is because of Will that I was not killed that night five years ago by a drunken neighbor whose son I had fooled around with. Apparently Charlie had let it slip to his father that I had slept with him. I think it may have been in a last-ditch effort to win some respect or approval from good old Dad.

Benjy was always going on and on to anyone who would listen about how he couldn't understand how any son of his could turn out to be such a pasty-faced wimp and how if, God forbid, his suspicion that Charlie might be queer was ever confirmed, he would take his head off with a shotgun.

Benjy himself had come back from the Mekong Delta missing more than just a chunk of his shoulder. His wits too were pretty much gone, and his favorite activity was to sit on his back porch with a shotgun across his lap and stare off into space looking for the Vietcong.

Charlie was an only child, and it's probably a good thing. But a lifetime of his father had made him a timid, mousy boy who was afraid to speak for fear that a solid whack upside his head would follow.

He could have been good-looking if he'd taken any care of himself. Instead his hair and skin were greasy and unkempt. He'd grown his blond hair somewhat long in an effort to hide his face from the world. His eyes were wide and surprised and brilliant green in color, really quite beautiful except for the way that they were forever darting around.

For some reason, I had always felt a certain tie to Charlie, who lived two houses down from us. Maybe it was because both of us had been fucked up by our fathers. Or maybe it was just that he was one of the only people I could tell was as hurt by life as I was. I didn't love him, but I did care for him, and that's why I didn't feel too bad messing around with him when we were both just thirteen. He discovered immediately that his dad was way off and that he was as straight as an arrow, though unsure of himself.

When I was fourteen, I decided we should just go ahead and have sex so we could figure out what all the fuss was about. I'd heard enough by then to be both curious and bored by the whole idea. So we did.

Charlie was my first time and, as it usually goes, it was disappointing. I liked it anyway, though, because I felt afterwards that he would probably be willing to do pretty much anything I wanted.

I did not caution him against telling anyone, because I didn't think it was necessary. Charlie did not really have friends in school and talked even less to his mother than to his father. She was a timid woman who was every bit as frightened of Benjy as Charlie was.

I can't say exactly how it happened, and I never asked Charlie, because, after that day in April, I never talked to him again. I think Charlie's dad must have been ragging on him about his clear-but-latent preference for boys when Charlie decided to convince him once and for all that he was straight. So he told him about me.

I know he wouldn't have done it if I had asked him to keep quiet or if he'd had any idea of the consequences.

9

Charlie's dear old Dad was far from delighted at the news and saw it as proof that his son was going to be something worse than wimpy or even gay; he was going to be promiscuous.

Benjy seemed to feel that this was heading Charlie, and therefore him, toward a whole world of trouble filled with unexpected pregnancies and lawsuits, with multiple women and child support, with food stamps and broken homes, and suddenly his fear that Charlie might be gay turned instead into a wish.

He came over to our house that night, roaring drunk, having decided that the best way to cure Charlie was to get rid of me, especially in case I was pregnant.

He banged into our house without warning. Mom was gone, probably, ironically, with another man. I knew she'd never been with Mr. Magee, and I wondered dimly at the time—and am almost sure now—if Magee himself weren't gay.

Anyway, I happened to be in the kitchen finishing up the dishes as he strode through our small living room. I heard his footsteps and turned around at the sink to see who it was.

Before I knew what was going on, I felt a hand grab my ponytail and force my face under the sudsy water, with the scum of grease floating on top. I managed to draw a breath before I went under, or I would have been a goner for sure.

I thrashed and flailed wildly and somehow managed to pull the plug on the sink. The water began to drain and, frustrated, Magee pulled me back out. Cursing, he started to drag me towards the table, still holding my hair, but tripped over some blocks that Tommy was playing with. He went sprawling, and Tommy began to bawl. Magee struck out and cracked Tommy on the head, causing him to scream even louder.

I took advantage of the situation and bolted through the living room and out the front door, screaming for all I was worth.

Jen had already come running from the yard, where she had been pushing Sarah on a rope swing, and I heard her scream too as she came through the back door into the kitchen where Magee was still yelling. He did not bother with Jen or Sarah, but came thundering after me. I'd made it to the porch when I felt his hand graze my back, and it was the jolt of terror that his touch sent through me that caused me to trip and fall down the steps of the front porch.

Magee swooped down on me like a vulture and pulled me by the hair again. He clutched me around my waist, and suddenly I felt the shaft of a knife pressed into the side of my neck. It was a switchblade. The blade was still in, but I knew, horribly and assuredly, that in a minute he would press the button and send it through one side of my throat and out the other.

I could no longer scream. But he didn't push the button just yet. Instead he began to murmur to me, right in my ear like some sort of perverse lover. Some things he said were nonsense, but some were about what should happen to girls like me.

The world seemed to have no sound but his voice.

Will and Jared burst through the door right then, one after the other, and saw the glint of the knife. Jared stood stock still, watching, but Will came rushing at us. I tried to tell him not to, terrified that this would make Magee press the button on the knife. But I could not make any noise come from my throat.

Then Jared yelled, "Stop!"

Will did so instantly. He retreated a few steps, eyeing Magee, and then pulled a pistol from his pocket.

I was surprised, and I sensed Magee stiffen.

Jared glanced from Will to the pistol to me, then back to the pistol, but he didn't move. Will was inching backwards, but as he did so, he raised the gun until it was pointing in Magee's direction.

I had no idea Will could shoot and thought he must be faking, trying to scare off Mr. Magee.

Then he fired the first shot.

I heard the bullet whiz past my left ear. My face was still pressed into the crook of Magee's arm, and he was bending down whispering in my right ear, right hand at my throat, left holding me firmly around the middle.

He stopped speaking then. He could tell that the shot had been a deliberate miss. Then Will aimed the gun again, but now he was studying us, letting

Magee soak in the fact that the next shot wouldn't be a miss. Jared remained frozen in place.

And just as suddenly as it had happened, it was all over.

The whole sequence of events took less than ten minutes. Magee released me and pocketed the knife, keeping his eyes fixed on Will and the pistol.

My knees gave way, and I collapsed to the ground. The world suddenly seemed to have sound again, too much of it. I heard sobbing and slowly came to realize that it was me. I had not cried that way in a long time, since before Dad left, and the noises I made were alien to me.

I felt someone lift me up and saw that it was Will. He carried me to the swing and held me, stroking my hair, and murmuring softly and soothingly. I had not felt that safe since I was very little and, in the midst of a bout of pneumonia, my father had cradled me and sung to me in a deep baritone.

I was dimly aware of other things happening. The girls crying, then quieting. The gun still lying on the porch where Will had flung it as he rushed to hold me. Jared crying after the others had stopped. Then, later, Mom coming home and panicking. Will reassuring her, still holding me. Her trying to put me to bed, but my refusing to go without Will. My sleeping next to him, waking up every hour or so to clutch him desperately and hear him reassure me that it was over and okay now.

I remember it all. I remember Will.

Will saved me from Benjy Magee, but, later on, he saved me from myself. I did not forget that incident with Magee quickly. In fact remembering it even now, five years later, brings bile up the back of my throat and makes me feel almost dizzy with horror.

In the nine or ten months that separated that day from the one when I nearly killed myself, I grew quieter than Jared and even less responsive. I stopped caring about my schoolwork and stopped talking to the few friends I had.

I didn't go around with many boys, and when I did, I made sure that they were nearly strangers to me. I'd seen what could happen with the ones I knew. I felt it was a lot safer to keep relationships basic, physical, and short. I found many guys who thought the same way.

I grew skinnier in a time when I should have been gaining curves all over. I didn't stop eating what food we had, but in a family where it was nearly always in short supply, skimping on what I did eat was not generally noticed or, if it was, was appreciated rather than punished. Food simply did not have any appeal to me. Nothing had any appeal for me. Not school, not friends, not the boys, not my own siblings—except for Will.

I don't know how much any of the others noticed, because I did not give them a chance to tell me if they did. It seemed to me that they worried about entirely the wrong things. If I came in late, Mom or

Jared or Will would always question me about who I was with or what I was doing. I would fight them and fight them, hurling vicious insults at them all.

According to me, Mom was no better and had done all the same things at my age; Jared cared more about his own reputation than about my life; and Will wasn't one to talk, because I knew what he did when, as so often happened, he wasn't at school.

What I didn't see then, but do see now, especially in light of what Will told me the night he died, was that Will had been on the same spiraling track. He too had stopped caring about everyone except—and I hate to admit this—Jared.

I never could love Jared, because I felt, as surely as if he had told me, that Will loved him more than he did me. I don't think it was a conscious choice he could make. When Will said that about our family, how we all refused to love Jared and loved him instead, how it wasn't something either boy could change, he might as well have been talking about me.

I wished for Will to love me as he did Jared, but I could not make it happen. I felt that Jared was blind to how deep and rare the attachment Will had for him was. To Jared it may have been commonplace, a way of life, but I saw it for what it really was—precious.

In the end, given what Will sacrificed for me, given how precious I became to him with Jared gone, I suppose I should feel vindicated, but at the time it only hurt me more. It only increased my loneliness and desperation. Will was the only one I loved. And he cared more for Jared than for me. It seemed as if the only thing that could have given my life meaning would not.

I slipped easily and silently into icy desolation. I began to wonder each day what it might feel like not to wake up. And soon it seemed a more promising prospect.

I began to save pills.

I knew even ordinary aspirin would do it if I took enough of them. I saved them slowly, one or two per day, so that it would not seem odd if the bottle emptied quickly. I saved thirty-six.

I planned to take them all, one after another, like the SweeTarts we sometimes got in our stockings when we were little. I was going to do it in the bathroom after Sarah and Jen had fallen asleep.

That night I lined up the tablets, one after another, on the countertop. I filled a glass with water and raised the first aspirin to my mouth. I hesitated, put down the aspirin, then went into Will's and Jared's room.

Will was lying awake, and I wondered if he had some sense that something would happen tonight. If I had started swallowing the tablets, would he have sensed that as well and rushed in to stop me?

I like to think that he would. It comforts me.

But as it happened, he was lying awake. I stood across the room in my ratty nylon nightshirt, my too-thin legs and bony elbows poking out. My stringy hair hung in my face, and I looked up only slowly to meet Will's intense brown eyes.

His eyes were a soulful, deep brown, so dark it

was almost impossible to distinguish his irises from his pupils. Jared's eyes were a piercing blue, and it was the one thing about their appearance that really distinguished them from each other.

"I wish I were dead," I said. I hadn't realized that I was going to say anything. "I really do."

The words were simple, but I thrust all the feelings I had kept inside for the past ten months into them, and they told Will everything. They told him that I felt that whatever others thought that I seemed to have going for me was all a lie. That I felt as though I didn't deserve anything good. That anyone who said they cared for me was lying. That I didn't deserve anyone's care or respect or, least of all, love.

That the world would be a better place without me in it.

Will heard all that in my words, I realize now, in large part because he had felt the same way. Yet for both of us there was a saving grace, a constant that could keep us intact. Jared was his and he, in turn, was mine. So when I went to him, I was really asking him to save me. And he knew it.

And he did.

I sat on the bed with him, and he rubbed my back in gentle circles, enveloping me in his arms, while I cried softly. I wasn't crying because I was sad. I was crying because I was relieved. I was relieved that now I would not kill myself.

His arms felt wonderfully strong, and I felt lost in them, although I knew logically that he was as thin as or even thinner than I was. The emotion was what mattered, and to me he felt invincible.

Will spoke after a bit, and his voice had just as many layers of feeling in it as mine had. He pulled away from me, and as he spoke, his eyes flashed with what looked like anger.

"Why don't you wish Dad were dead? You didn't do anything. None of us did. If anyone should be dead, it should be him for leaving us."

Then he also cried, and I held him as tightly as he held me.

I was relieved. I had him, and now I had life. And he had me. And, a small triumphal part of me whispered, *Jared was not a part of it*. That was the night that things took a turn in so many ways. A new distance formed between Jared and Will, and a new connection formed between Will and me.

I believe now that Will resolved then and there to let Jared go and was preparing himself for the sacrifice, pushing Jared away in the hope that it would make his leaving easier for both of them.

I heard Will say more than once on the night he died that Jared gave him his life and he was using it for his family. But what I did not have the courage to tell Will was that he had already saved my life.

It was unfair, really, that Will should have sacrificed himself twice. But he did. So now I have my life.

And what am I doing with it? Do I want to go on living at home, somewhere between a fantasy in which my brother is alive and a reality in which he lies buried in an anonymous small-town grave?

For a while, I hated Mom for being what I thought

of as unnecessarily dramatic, but I took comfort in the belief that this was a sign that Will's plan had worked. This meant that Will had not died for nothing, our traveling would stop, and we would get to stay at home and work at rebuilding normal lives.

At some point between September, when Mom began talking again, and October, when we returned to our house, I believed that this return to normalcy would be possible. Now it is February. It is dark, it is cold, and I no longer believe that.

Not that I don't want to believe it. It might have been possible, except for one thing. Will was right about Jared. He did return home, and almost right away. By the end of July, he showed up on Grandma's porch, looking taller and fuller than he had five years earlier, but with the same startling eyes.

Jared was just as quiet, just as patient, and just as kind as ever. But somehow his presence made life nearly unbearable for me. Returning to the house— our house—has only made it worse.

I cannot feel that I am at home without Will.

That has brought the reality of his death closer to me than anything else. In this house, where we lived together from when we were in diapers until we were teenagers, his absence is more noticeable to me than Dad's or even Jared's ever was.

It is as though his presence seeped into every chair and table, every inch of ratty carpet and stained linoleum, every pore of the cheap paneled walls, every board of the rickety porches. Memories assault me with a nearly physical force and sometimes I am so overwhelmed that I sit down wherever I am to cry.

The creak of the bedsprings in the boys' room where Tommy now sleeps in Will's place, the whisper of the water in the kitchen sink, the swish of the curtains open for a breeze on hot nights, they all seem to be signs of Will, and each time he is not there, my heart is bruised a little more. Sometimes when I hear the screen door click, I think it's him. I want him here so desperately that sometimes I think he must be.

Jared knows what I am feeling. I can tell he knows, and I can tell he is just as torn apart as I am. I feel that, especially at a time like this, we should be able to reach out and bond over the brother we both loved so passionately and help one another. But if anything, Will's death seems to have driven us an even greater distance apart.

That Jared looks so much like Will is hard for me. Often, I feel that I am seeing a ghost or, more painfully, that it was all a nightmare and Will is still alive. But then Jared turns, and I see his eyes, and I know the truth. I cannot love the boy who embodies that truth.

And I cannot return to normal as long as I am here.

This is the reason that I am leaving, not because I do not love my family, not because I think they would be better off without me, but because I know that I cannot begin to live again until I am without them. I have to leave.

I've got a plan. I know where I'm going. I'm going to find the only person I know who embodies what

I loved in Will. I'm going to find the only other boy I've ever felt I could come close to loving.

And I'm leaving tonight.

David 2001/1981

She just showed up and knocked on my door.

It was raining that night, February rain, the worst kind. Even in Alabama it was cold by February, and every once in a while, we would see some snow. But this time it wasn't snowing, not quite.

The sky was spitting a ceaseless, steady rain. The rain felt as sharp as needles and colder than ice, yet it still wasn't sleet. It was the worst kind of rain on the worst kind of night when, after three years of nothing, she showed up and knocked on my door.

By 1981, I wasn't working in the real estate office or living in Melville anymore. I had moved a little farther north to a larger town called St. James. I worked days in the public library fetching and carrying, doing more grunt work than anything, but I enjoyed the proximity to books. Five nights a week, I worked in the local tavern. Lately I'd considered quitting that second job to earn some kind of degree from St. James Community College. That rainy February night was one of my nights off from the bar, and I had the course catalogue open in my lap.

All the doors and windows of my tiny frame house were closed against the gale, and to save money, all my lights were off. I was sitting in the living room in a squashy armchair reading by the glow of the fire in the fireplace. Each time I lit a fire, I was mildly surprised that it didn't demolish the shabby little house. I went on tempting fate, because the flickering flames made the room cozy and relaxing.

I was settled enough at my jobs that I had adopted a cat. I called him Socrates, a throwback to my days of high ambition, as well as an allusion to his amusing know-it-all air, even though the real Socrates, unlike my cat, was wise enough to know that he knew nothing.

Socrates was curled up on the arm of my chair, and I was paging through the course catalogue, musing about what I could take to best advance myself. I was wondering about how I could get off the path that, like an idiot, I had rashly committed myself to in 1977.

I had begun to realize that I wasn't necessarily predestined for a dead-end life, as I had led myself to think. I had started feeling angry at my younger self for letting the incident with Amy affect me so profoundly as to jeopardize the rest of my life.

I had resolved not to let any similar situation do the same thing. I was prepared to pick up my life once more and hold it together, come what may.

I had a beer in my hand, but it was the first of only two that I would drink. I never drank while I was working at the bar, because I had to be sober to deal with the real drunks, but on my nights off, I usually had only two beers. Even on an unusually stressful day, I would never, ever exceed four.

That is how on-track to recovery I was. The year 1980-1981 was the best time I'd had since my days of marching with my sister Maggie.

And then came that knock.

2

I have never been lucky, and looking back it seems like her arriving just then was like a personal *fuck-you* from fate. I wish to God I had just slammed the door and dashed right back to the road-not-taken.

Instead, when I heard the knock, I looked up suddenly enough to make Socrates jump, then bristle in surprise. He glared at me through half-closed eyes, then began to lick his paw as if nothing had happened.

The knock sounded again, and this time I stood up.

If I were writing fiction, I would say that I felt a thrill of dread, a sense of foreboding that warned me not to open that door.

But I had no such feelings.

I was simply surprised and puzzled. None of my few friends was due over, and I could hardly imagine a spontaneous visit on a night as horrible as this one. I hadn't ordered out for food and hadn't planned on trying to get any of my girlfriends to join me for company as I often did. I was just too tired. My week had been particularly hard, and the reason I was looking at the catalogue was that I could not imagine working another year as a bartender. I hated dealing with all the pathetic drunks. I could not have imagined that soon I would be one of them.

I moved automatically to my door. I wasn't afraid it would be a murderer or a robber. The world had already begun to turn more universally unpleasant than it had been for most of my life, but we did not feel it as much in small towns like St. James.

Besides, I had matured and put on some muscle. I was six-two, and while I was no martial arts expert, I could handle myself. I got plenty of practice, because I often had to act as a bouncer on weekends.

I turned on the light in the living room, opened the door, and peered out into the darkness.

3

Amy stood in the rain, her face pale in the light spilling from the opened door.

I would be a colossal liar if I said that I hadn't even thought of her in years. The truth is that I had thought of her constantly nearly every day for two years before she began slowly to leave my mind. In the last year, there had been days when I would not think of her at all, but others when I could think of almost nothing else.

I was often angry with myself for letting Amy dictate the path my life took. Yet even in my most reflective moments, I could not see any other way it could have gone, given how I felt about her. I am utterly certain that I loved her. But I am just as certain that she did not love me, at least not that first time.

Why that was the case I still don't know, and I'm sick of trying to figure it out. I think perhaps that she was not even capable of love at that time. But I loved her whether she was or not, and when she let me down, it tore me apart. It hurt me so badly that I didn't let myself feel anything for anyone, until a full two years later.

That episode with someone I met at the real estate office was scarcely more than a schoolboy crush. But at least it was something. After a couple of years of feeling hollow, even that was a comfort. It meant I was getting over her. It meant I was getting better.

And then she showed up.

I didn't recognize her at first.

Not because I didn't remember her from 1977, because I had thought of her so often and for so long that I could have reconstructed every particle of her from memory. My memory was perfect, but she didn't look at all like my memory.

She was so changed that I mistook her for a stranger. Standing on my doorstep, she looked down at her feet, her matted hair turned nearly black from the frigid rain. Her clothes were sodden and hung off her body in heavy folds. The parts of her legs that I could see emerging from her dark skirt were stick thin and covered in goose bumps.

Even though the night was biting cold, she wore only a short-sleeved white blouse, and I saw bruises running up and down both arms. Her nipples were small, hard knobs that pressed against the fabric of the blouse, but nothing about her appearance was sexually attractive. Her whole body seemed to have shrunk and lost its vitality.

She raised her face to me, pushing back her sodden hair, and even though the light was dim, I saw a bruise across her cheek and heavy, dark circles under her still startlingly blue eyes.

"David." She said my name almost as a sob.

She spoke it not as a question, or an exclamation, or even a statement, but as an expression freighted with recognition, sadness, desperation, and above all a sense of grateful relief.

She stepped forward and fell into my arms, and although I had imagined this sort of situation a hundred times over on the nights when I would lie awake and miss her, the reality was bitter and confusing.

A hundred thoughts passed through my mind, and even more emotions ran through my heart as I held her to my chest. Her body shook with cold or sobs or maybe both.

I wanted to coo to her and tell her everything would be all right, yet I also wanted to scream at her and demand to know how she could show her face after hurting me the way she had.

I had the urge to hold her close, but I also had the urge to send her back from wherever she had come from, no questions asked. In the end, I did what I would have done for anyone in that weather. I took her inside and shut the door behind us.

This sealed my fate.

4

She straightened up a bit after her initial collapse, and something of the old Amy showed in that. I was pleased to notice it, even in my confusion.

She walked unsteadily toward the fire and, holding her hands to it, turned to look at me. Socrates had sprung up from the chair and run toward the kitchen. He paused on the threshold, held there by his curiosity.

I looked at him looking at her, and realized with amusement that I was doing the same thing. I was halfway to the staircase that would take me away from the living room, but I had paused to stare at Amy.

Well, we know about curiosity and the cat, I thought.

"You were hard to find," Amy said. Her tone was accusing, but she didn't seem to expect a response. That was too bad, because the hurt, furious part of me was aching to give her one.

"I was pretty sure you wouldn't still be living in Melville, but I never guessed you'd be working at a library. Maybe I should have known, what with philosophy and all … ."

Amy trailed off and looked at me, and I felt angry, but also full of admiration. Either way it was daring of her to bring up that night, the one that had made me furious and thrown me off my path, the one that had left me unable to feel anything for years. To bring it up first thing upon seeing me, especially given the state she was in, took a lot of nerve.

My initial thought after the shock of seeing her was that she had run away from some kind of abusive relationship. *Boyfriend or husband, probably*, I thought, as I saw the bruise on her cheek and the ones on her arms. *He's been careful not to do anything that would send her to the hospital, but she does look banged up.*

But even as I was thinking this, I found it hard to believe. I remembered Amy saying to me that night, as I stammered and tried to explain that I hadn't meant to knock her down. *I know you don't pull shit like that*, she had said. *Think I'd have hung around you more than a day if you did?* So I could not picture Amy being with someone who abused her. But, I told myself, people change.

As I looked more closely at her arms, however, they looked less like marks from being grabbed roughly and more like … *junkie tracks*. The words sprang into my mind, and I felt instantly sure that my instinct was right.

I'd seen my share of junkie tracks in the bar, in college, and even on those peace marches of long ago, and I recognized them as easily as I would have recognized a black eye.

Sure of my guess, I moved closer to Amy. With new eyes, I assessed her rail-thin body and the dark hollows under her eyes. She sensed something in my gaze and stopped speaking. She might have been studying me the way I was studying her. I will never know, because at that moment her façade crumbled.

She gave a high-pitched laugh, then looked down at the carpet.

"I can see what you're thinking, but I want you to know I'm not high right now." She then began to speak in an unbroken, nearly incomprehensible stream of words, her voice higher and thinner than usual. "I haven't been high in a long time, mostly because I haven't had the money or the time." She looked up at me. "So, David, right now I am stone cold sober and that is making this whole mess even more horrible."

Her words resonated in my mind, almost exact echoes of those she had spoken the night of our horrible fight. The night of the miscarriage. I suddenly realized that she was still talking in that same endless stream of high-pitched words.

"... could since then, but it was him, David. He just went crazy, and then he was so scared and he wanted me to help him, but I just wanted to run away, because he was scaring me more than anything I've ever seen when strung out. So I ran but he caught me leaving and hit me a couple of times, but I made it. And when I got out, I didn't have any idea what to do. All I could think of was how you'd wanted to help before, and all I could think of was you. So I'm here finally, Davy, I'm here. Please help me ... please, please, please, please ... ."

Her pleading suddenly became a high-pitched gasping, as if she were suffocating, then the gasping turned into shrill laughter.

I watched, wide-eyed and terrified. I had never seen anyone fall to pieces so utterly. When Amy and I had suffered through our emotional turmoil, she had been in control. Even with the vestiges of the unborn baby trickling down her legs, she had remained calm enough to give me instructions.

Now I wasn't sure if she still knew where she was. Her eyes were on me, but they were unfocused and staring. I did the only thing I could think of and slapped her unbruised cheek with the flat of my hand.

Her head jerked to one side with the force of my slap, and a scabbed-over gash beside her ear I hadn't noticed opened up. Blood began to run down her cheek.

She was still staring at me, but the laughing had stopped. I then noticed that her nose was also bleeding. Maybe the result of another old injury I had opened up, because I hadn't hit her nose.

We stared at one another for what seemed minutes. Then she murmured what I took to be "I knew you would" and collapsed into my arms, unconscious.

5

Time seemed to slow down as Amy's full weight pulled at me.

As if observing her from above, I saw her thin body become limp, her head loll to one side, and her knees sag at an unnatural angle.

To keep her from hitting the floor, I placed one hand across her chest and wrapped my arm around her middle. Her hair fell over her head, and her eyes rolled up so that only the whites were showing.

I staggered more from surprise than because of her weight. She couldn't weigh more than a hundred pounds, even though she was soaking wet.

I stretched her out in front of the fire and tucked the pillow from my chair under her head, turning her head to the side in case she vomited. Something I had learned to do in dealing with passed-out drunks in the bar. I put two fingers on her neck above her jaw and felt her pulse beating away. That relieved me some, although her heart did seem to be going awfully fast.

I left Amy where she was to get my first aid kit out of the garage. In my hurry, I almost stumbled over Socrates. He spat at me, and I swore back, causing him to streak for his favorite sulking place behind the reading chair in my bedroom.

I ran to the kitchen and jerked open the door into the garage. I flipped the switch for the overhead light, but nothing happened. I glanced behind me, and seeing that the kitchen light was on, I realized that the bulb had burned out.

Returning to the kitchen I cracked my hip on the green Formica table and swore to myself. I bent down beside the sink and pulled opened the junk drawer. After fumbling around with the wrenches, screwdrivers, and a claw hammer, I found the flashlight and switched it on.

I located my first aid kit right where it was supposed to be, on the top shelf above the worktable in the garage. A layer of dust covered the Red Cross emblem on the front of the white metal box, but the lid was still latched, so I felt confident that the contents were still safe to use.

I unlatched the lid on my kitchen table, sending dust motes floating in the light. The silk-covered glass ampules of ammonium carbonate were in a small cardboard box, and I took the whole box with me as I rushed back to the living room.

At first I didn't notice Amy, then I saw that she was sitting on the floor in front of the fireplace. The dim light concealed her bruises and the blood on her face.

I thought she should have remained lying down until I could tell whether she was seriously ill. But I was also annoyed that I had scared my cat, banged my hip on the kitchen table, and been scared for her, only to find her looking so normal. It made me feel foolish, but I still had sense enough to recognize that this was not the time to be petty.

I knelt down beside her.

"You okay?" I asked. "I think maybe you fainted."

Amy seemed not to hear me. She stared straight into the fire, rocking slightly, her knees drawn up to her chest. I wondered if she was deliberately ignoring me.

"Amy? Amy, are you okay?" I changed my position so that I could face her directly.

She still didn't answer, and I became alarmed.

I pulled out the box of smelling salts that I had stuck in my pocket and took out one of the silk-covered ampules. I broke it open with my fingers and held it directly under her nose.

The strong odor of ammonia burned my nose, and I had to pull back. Amy's only response was to turn her head to the side and keep rocking back and forth.

At least she can move, I thought.

I dropped the ampule on the floor and shined my flashlight into Amy's eyes. The pupils instantly contracted, so her involuntary nervous system seemed to be functioning.

Yet she wasn't speaking or responding to my voice. I didn't think she was aware of me at all.

The basic Red Cross first-aid course I had taken as part of my training for the bar job hadn't covered any situation remotely like this one. I was utterly confounded.

I did the only other thing I could think of to help. I rushed up to my bedroom and grabbed a dark blue sweatshirt, matching sweatpants, and a pair of thick gray socks. If I couldn't get Amy to snap out of whatever state she was in, I could at least make sure she didn't die from hypothermia.

"Hey, Amy?" I said. "I'm going to take off your wet stuff, and I've got some dry clothes for you."

I hadn't expected her to respond, and she didn't. Yet explaining things to her made me feel better about what I was doing. If there was a chance of her understanding me, I felt I ought to tell her.

I knelt down and began to unbutton her shirt. To remove it, I had to pull her arms off her knees, and she let me do it without protest. Her knees stayed upright, but her arms fell limp by her sides.

I felt like I was undressing a mannequin or a rag doll.

As I finally pulled off her shirt, I had to stifle a gasp. I could see all of her ribs through her skin. Between skin and bone, there seemed to be no flesh.

As I slipped an arm around her to move her to one side, I saw a line of dark, irregular spots along her back. I found that puzzling, then I realized that she was so thin that her vertebrae had rubbed bruises on her skin.

Working quickly, I slipped the blue sweatshirt over her head, anxious to conceal the sight. I gently eased her down and put the pillow under her head. Lifting her legs, I pulled off her skirt, but left on her tattered panties, feeling that it wouldn't be right to take away her privacy and dignity. I slid on the sweatpants, working on one leg, then the other. I was shocked to see how emaciated she was. Her waist was at most a third the size of mine and despite the elastic in the waistband, the sweatpants wouldn't stay in place if she stood up.

I got the ball of twine out of the junk drawer in the kitchen and wrapped a length of it around her waist. I cinched the twine tight and tied the ends together in a bow. I finished dressing her by pulling the heavy gray socks over her feet.

I rubbed her arms and legs, hoping to warm her up. Noticing how wet her hair was, I went back upstairs and brought down two towels and my hairbrush.

Pulling her into a sitting position, I leaned her back against my knee and used one of the towels to dry her long hair. As I brushed it, I noticed that it had become thinner and wondered how long it had been since she had a real meal. I didn't have any ribbons to tie back her hair, so I wrapped it in the dry towel and did my best to secure the ends in a sort of turban.

It bothered me that she was so thin and that her skin was so bruised and cold. I decided there was nothing else I could do until morning or until Amy came out of whatever state she was in.

I went back upstairs and brought down an old patchwork quilt that my grandmother had given me before she died. I wrapped it around Amy and carried her, light as a sleeping child, upstairs to my bedroom at the back of the house. I put her on her side so that if she threw up she wouldn't choke. I then tucked the quilt around her and sat in the large, cushioned armchair at the end of the bed.

Socrates jumped on my lap, and we settled down to wait for morning.

6

I didn't know what to expect as I sat beside Amy and watched the pink-orange glow outside my bedroom window turn into bright sunlight.

During the seven or eight hours I had watched over her, I checked her pulse six or eight times, just to be sure she was still alive. Even so, she was so still and corpse-like that I was more than worried. I was scared shitless.

I was terrified as much for myself as for her. What if she had some weird contagious disease? Was I going to get it too? If hadn't appeared yet, but even it had, I couldn't have been more frightened than I already was.

I had no way to tell what I was dealing with. I had gotten her blood on my hands, and even though I had scrubbed it off, would soap and water be enough to disinfect whatever germ she might be carrying? I told myself I was being overdramatic, but that didn't keep my heart from racing or my throat from tightening with panic.

I thought about taking her to the local clinic, but I didn't think they would be able to do much for her. Also, St. James was a small town, and if I showed up with a strange girl with needle tracks on her arms, we could both end up in jail.

Even if we didn't, I would likely lose my jobs, and my attempt to put my past life behind me and invent a new one would come to an end. I wasn't sure I was up to another effort.

But if Amy died, I would have to call the police and explain why she was in my house and hope that they didn't think that I had killed her. So maybe I should take her to the clinic and hope that the consequences wouldn't be as bad as I thought.

I vacillated between hoping Amy would eventually wake up and putting her in my car and taking her to the clinic. The only person I could think of who could help with this kind of decision was my mother.

I decided to call her.

7

My parents were still living in Melville. They had slowed down a bit, but they were still sipping unsweetened iced tea on back porches with their friends in the summer and exchanging cookies with them in the winter.

I always got on well with my parents, despite what as a teenager I thought of as their small-town ways. They had always been ready to help me, and given the peculiar and maybe catastrophic situation I was in with Amy, I needed practical advice.

And no one was better at giving practical advice than my mother.

She grew up as the oldest of nine kids in one of the few Catholic families in her little Alabama town. She was hardly more than kindergarten age when she started taking care of her younger siblings, giving bottles, changing diapers, bathing, and being an all-around little mother. As she grew older and her siblings grew more numerous, she took on more responsibilities.

She could diagnose chicken pox with one eye, while seeing to her mending with the other; stir the grits with her left hand, while cradling the newest baby with her right.

My mother was not particularly sweet or patient, but she was extraordinarily capable. Throughout my life, that had served me better than sweetness or patience would have, although I can't deny that I sometimes wished for her to be a little softer. But my father had cornered the market on sweet and patient, so as parents they balanced each other nicely.

It was because of my mother's practicality that she allowed Maggie and me to go off and join protest marches when Brian was killed. She knew that we'd both hero-worshipped him all our lives, knew that a vast anger was inside both of us because of his senseless death, and sensed that it would be wrong to stop us from expressing that anger by protesting against injustice.

Her practicality also kept her from saying anything negative about my father's whittling. He whittled whenever he had a problem, and you could tell the size of the problem by the size of what he produced while he was thinking about it. During the years after Brian died, he carved a block of walnut the size of a foot locker into the beautiful figure of a wood nymph. He then stored it in the attic, maybe not wanting to be reminded of what it represented.

I suddenly needed my mother's practical advice more than I needed anything. So I grabbed a handful of change out of the jar on top of my bureau, gave Amy a glance to see if she was still breathing, and climbed into my 1972 Pinto.

I drove the two miles to the Texaco station and parked opposite the pay phone, which was near the restrooms at the side of the building. It was the phone I always used to keep in touch with my parents, so I knew that it worked.

I dropped in four quarters, then six dimes, listening to the different tones as the coins dropped. When I got the dial tone, I dialed what I still thought of as my home number.

Although it was only six-thirty in the morning, I knew my mother would have been up for at least an hour. Sure enough, I wasn't disappointed. She answered on the third ring.

She said hello in the crisp voice she used when she wasn't sure who she was talking to. It was business-like, but not unfriendly.

"Hello, Momma. It's me." I tried not to sound upset.

"David, is something wrong? You're calling awfully early."

I heard the concern in her voice, but it wasn't anxiety or panic. She trusted me to take care of myself the way she had taught me, so she didn't immediately assume that I must be in the hospital or in jail.

But she did want to know if something was wrong.

"Well, no. I mean, yes there is, but not exactly with me. I don't want to tell you now, but can you come down today?"

I didn't see anybody close enough to eavesdrop, but people were starting to pull into the station for gas. At any moment, somebody might come to use the restroom or to try to use the phone.

"Davy, if it's that important, tell me what it is. I don't want to make a three-hour drive for nothing. And I'm supposed to watch Ida Salworthy's kids so she can go to see her doctor."

"Momma, I'm calling from the pay phone at the Texaco station."

"What is it that you can't say it in public?"

She sounded a little worried now, and I thought I knew why. After growing up with so many siblings, she never wanted one of her kids to be burdened with many offspring. So despite her Catholic upbringing, she approved of birth control. I guessed she was afraid I was about to become a father.

"You remember Amy, don't you?"

My parents had never met Amy, but they knew that, like me, she had gone to Joe Conway's parties. They also knew that I had continued to see her at LSU and that she had hurt me badly, even though I had never shared any of the details. They had never brought up her name, and this was the first time I had.

"I certainly do. Does the problem have to do with her?"

"Yes, but it's not what I suspect you're thinking."

"What is it then?"

"She showed up at my house last night."

"Why do you want me to come because of that?"

"I haven't seen or spoken to her in three years. Then last night she showed up all ... beaten up." I wasn't about to mention the needle marks. "I was talking to her, then she fainted or went into a coma. She's breathing and her eyes are open, but she won't wake up."

"I'll come down," my mother said. "Your daddy can watch Ida's kids. I should be there by 10:30."

"Thank you, Momma."

"Goodbye, Davy."

She said this very softly, and I realized that I had probably sounded hysterical. Not surprising, because that is the way I felt.

8

As I hung up the phone, I felt a wave of relaxation pass through me. I was so relieved that for a moment I almost forgot about Amy lying in bed in my house.

The moment passed, and I got back in my car and headed for home. I caught a glance from Homer, the station's owner, and waved to him. On a normal day, I would have gone inside, got a Milky Way out of the candy machine, and made small talk about the weather or the price of gas, but now I didn't have time for ordinary things.

When I got home, Socrates met me in the kitchen and gave a couple of loud meows to remind me that I hadn't fed him yet. But I needed to check on Amy first, and I hurried up the stairs.

She looked the same as she did when I left her.

I put my fingers on her neck to check her pulse and found that it was still strong and regular. I noticed a dark stain on the bottom sheet and realized that she had wet the bed. I took this as a good sign, because it meant that her body was still functioning. Now and then, she blinked, and I took that to be another good sign.

I thought about changing the sheet, but I decided that would take too much effort. Instead, I got another towel out of the bathroom, raised her hips and pushed the towel under her. At least she wouldn't have to lie on a wet mattress.

I wet a washcloth with warm water, squeezed it out, then used it to wash her face. I cleaned off the dried drool at the corners of her mouth and gently wiped her eyes.

Figuring there was nothing more I could do, I went downstairs and opened a can of Friskies. I dumped it into Socrates's bowl and set it down in the corner by his water dish. He rushed toward it as he were starving and hadn't been fed in days. Unlike some cats, Socrates was not a finicky eater.

I glanced at my watch and saw that it was eight-fifteen, which meant I was fifteen minutes late for my library job. I had completely forgotten that I had to go to work.

I got back into the Pinto and drove back to the Texaco station, parking in exactly the same place as last time.

I dropped two nickels in the phone's coin slot and dialed Mark Tanner's personal number. Mark was Head Librarian and a decent person.

"I'm not going to be able to make it in today," I told Mark. "I need to take a sick day, but I'm not the one who's sick. My little sister is here for a visit, and I think she might have pneumonia. Or maybe just the flu. Anyway, I can't leave her by herself."

"We can struggle along without you for a while," Mark said. "I've got a couple of sisters myself, so I understand about family duty. Try some hot lemonade, it helps break up the congestion."

"That's a good idea," I said. "I'll be back as soon as I can."

It wasn't my night to work at the tavern, so I was now free to do whatever I needed to do.

Homer wasn't in sight as I drove away. If he had

seen me using the phone a second time, I'm certain he would have had questions. That's part of small-town life.

9

I glanced at Amy and saw that she had shifted her position on the bed. That struck me as yet another good sign.

I took a shower and changed into a fresh pair of khakis and a blue-striped shirt. I sat back down in the chair at the foot of the bed and tried to read a Fitzgerald short story, but I found I couldn't concentrate. I still found Amy's staring but apparently unseeing eyes unnerving.

A little before ten-thirty, I heard two sharp raps on my front door. Then came the third knock. The pattern was as characteristic of my mother as her gold-rimmed bifocals, and I associated both of them with her for as far back as I could remember.

As I opened the front door and saw my mother standing in the pale morning light, a wave of relief swept through me. I took a deep breath and sighed.

She was wearing a tailored blue woolen skirt and a light blue blouse. Her navy pea coat was buttoned and her hands were hidden in its slit pockets. The pea coat was a favorite of hers and had been mended many times, although none of the repairs was visible. Despite the cold weather, she was wearing low heels with open toes and sling backs.

She was getting to be old enough to be called elderly, but she resisted any temptation to wear sensible shoes. Nor did she dye her hair. It hung loose around her face and was almost completely gray. Yet on her the color seemed natural and becoming, as if she had long ago decided that silver was her best color.

I was so relieved to see my mother that I almost started crying. I reached out to hug her, and although she seemed surprised, she gave me a quick squeeze.

"So how is she?" My mother stepped inside and closed the door after her. "Any change?" Then giving me no chance to answer, she said. "That was a long drive, and I need some coffee."

She walked past me and headed into the kitchen. She knew where I kept the coffee, because during the year or so I had lived in the house, she had visited me a couple of times.

I was happy to let her take charge, and five minutes later, I was sitting at the green Formica kitchen table drinking a cup of coffee she had added milk and sugar to before putting it in front of me. Years had passed since I had my coffee any way except black, but I didn't say anything. At my first sip, I found that the coffee tasted very good and wondered why I had stopped drinking it that way.

My mother sat down across from me, then stared at me over the rim of her cup. She was clearly asking me for details.

"I told you on the phone about all that I know," I

said. "Amy showed up last night in the rain. She was wet and cold, and I noticed she had some bruises. So I thought that maybe she was running away from an abusive boyfriend or husband."

"That's it?" My mother gave me a questioning look.

I suspected she thought that I was hiding something from her. Like maybe that Amy was pregnant, even if I wasn't the father.

"It's all I know," I said. "I asked if she was okay, and she said she knew that I'd take care of her. She sounded hysterical, then she passed out. I went to the garage to get the smelling salts out of the first aid kit, and when I got back, she was just staring into space."

"Her eyes were open?"

"Yeah, but she was totally unresponsive. And the smelling salts didn't wake her up. So I put some warm clothes on her and carried her upstairs and put her to bed."

My hands felt numb, and I cradled my mug of coffee, enjoying its warmth. The morning was cold and the gas heater never raised the temperature of the house to a comfortable level.

"And she's been there ever since," I added.

My mother considered me for a moment then seemed to decide that I wasn't holding anything back. She finished her coffee, put her cup in the sink, and got up from the table.

"Let me take a look at her," she said.

10

The first thing my mother did was what I had done many times—checked Amy's pulse. She put her hand flat on Amy's forehead to check for fever.

She then pulled back the covers. Seeing the green towel under Amy's hips, she nodded in approval. I didn't mention that I had been late in putting it there.

"Low-level coma," my mother said. "Probably from a combination of being cold and wet and whatever shock she experienced that made her come to see you."

"You've seen this before?" I had thought it was only shock, but I had wondered why Amy didn't come out of it.

"She looks like my sister Meg did when she fell through the ice on the pond. I thought she would never wake up, and the hours before my mother came home were some of the worst in my life."

"Do we have to take her to a hospital?"

"No, we can take care of her. Now go fill up your bathtub with hot water. Not scalding, but hot as you can stand."

"Wouldn't cold water wake her up?" I felt relieved that my mother had a plan, but I couldn't stifle my skepticism.

"We need to get her blood circulating again," my mother said. "Hot water will dilate her veins and arteries, and with any luck, her brain will respond."

"Makes sense," I said, feeling that it was something I should have thought of.

I went into the bathroom and turned on the hot water faucet. I let the water run until it felt hot against my hand, then I put in the white rubber stopper.

Kneeling beside the tub, I dipped my hand in the water from time to time to check the temperature. When the water got too hot for comfort, I turned on the cold faucet. I filled the tub about three-quarters full, then turned off both faucets.

I was grateful that my mother knew how to handle the situation, because now no one would ever have to know that Amy was here or that we had a history that was so painful.

Yet now that I look back at that time, it seems like it was the point at which everything in my life could have been put right again, if only I had taken Amy to a hospital, instead of treating her at home. But just then, I was relieved that I was able to keep her out of sight, so that the people I knew in the town wouldn't find out about her.

Ironically, I never stopped to consider that a conscious Amy might be an even bigger problem than an unconscious one.

By the time I got back to the bedroom, my mother had stripped off Amy's clothes and dropped them on the floor. I was relieved to see that Amy was still covered with a sheet.

"Let's carry her to the bathtub," my mother said. "I'll take her feet, and you pick her up by the shoulders."

My mother pulled back the sheet, leaving Amy completely exposed. I felt my face flush with embarrassment. I was standing with my mother looking at the naked body of my ex-girlfriend, someone I had slept with dozens of times and possibly had gotten pregnant. Some things boys just don't want to share with their mothers.

I was again struck by how skeletal Amy's body had become. My mother seemed to have noticed it for the first time. She raised a hand to her mouth, and I heard her sharp intake of breath.

I looked at her, confused by her reaction.

She met my gaze, and I saw that her eyes were misted with tears. Their brilliant blue appeared intensified, and behind the film of tears, I thought I could detect layer upon layer of things that had always been hidden from me. Within the depths of her eyes, images of all the hurtful things my mother had seen in her life seemed to be reflected. Images that she kept locked away and never talked about.

Her eyes had looked that way when the Army Notification Team, with their crisp uniforms and polished brass, had come to our door and relayed the news of Brian's death.

The thought occurred to be that maybe her eyes looked this way only when she had to open the vault in her mind to add yet another piercing pain. And that this was one of those times.

Neither of us spoke, but as we stared at each other over Amy's naked body, my mother gave an almost imperceptible shudder.

"How long has she been like this?" Her left hand trembled as she gestured toward Amy, her voice so thin and tight that I didn't recognize it.

I remained quiet for a moment, puzzled by why my mother was so affected by Amy's condition. She had never met Amy, and she didn't like what she had heard about her back in Melville. Yet the only other time I had seen her so unguarded, so emotional, was on that Tuesday in late September when the Army Notification Team came about Brian.

I now see that it was this moment that led my mother into something like an alliance with Amy. Not that they were ever in a war against me, but these two important women in my life appeared to become united in something I couldn't fathom. Perhaps it was some sisterhood of anguish to which I could never belong nor even hope to understand.

I sensed that my mother at that moment felt more than sympathy for Amy's pain that day—she felt Amy's pain as if it were her own. The moment passed, and Amy was not even conscious, but my mother's reaction significantly altered the course of my life.

"Since about eight last night," I said at last.

My mother blinked, and the windows through which I had glimpsed some of the concealed sorrows of her life closed up. Now her eyes had regained their usual hue of polished agate.

We lifted Amy's inert body off the bed and awkwardly carried her into the bathroom, with me in the lead, backing my way through the bedroom door.

The air in the bathroom was moist, and steam was still rising off the water in the bathtub.

"Ease her in," my mother said.

My mother put Amy's feet and legs into the hot water, and I then slipped in the upper part of her body. I held onto her head so that she wouldn't slide under the water and choke.

For a very long moment I thought that immersing Amy in the hot water wouldn't work.

Then Amy's eyelids fluttered, once, twice, then repeatedly. Her eyes lost their glazed, staring look. They seemed to come alive, and their dark blue color seemed to sparkle in the light of the bathroom.

Her mouth stretched into a startled O, and she began to struggle, her legs and arms splashing water onto the floor.

"Amy, you're okay," I said. "You are okay."

Supporting her head with my right hand, I moved to the side of the tub so that she could see me.

"David," she said, as soon as she saw my face. Her lips formed the start of a smile.

I lifted her out of the tub and sat her on the toilet seat. My mother draped a beach towel over her shoulders, and I wrapped it around her. The towel, with its images of a blue ocean, a jaunty red boat, and a denim sky filled with white sea birds, pictured a world that resembled in no detail my steamy bathroom with its walls of pink blistered paint.

Leaning over, I pulled Amy to me and hugged her tightly. I was relieved and glad that she was alive. Glad that her voice still worked. Glad to have her back in my arms, in just the way I had imagined during all the years since she had left me.

Amy wrapped her arms around my hips and hugged me back, harder than I imagined she was able. She leaned against me, and her wet hair soaked through my shirt.

This is like some strange pagan ceremony, I thought.

"It's all going to be okay now." She murmured the words in such a low voice that I doubt my mother heard them.

I tried to pull away, but Amy continued to cling to me.

While I held her and she held me, my mother wrapped a blanket around both of us. The February wind seeping through the leaky window was already lowering the temperature of the bathroom, and the blanket was warm.

Paul 2003

My feet send up puffs of cold dust as I wind my way back home, not taking the fastest route, but following the twisted back roads of my neighborhood, kicking up the dirt and thinking.

On this Louisiana February night, it's fixing to rain. You can feel it in the winter too, though it's not the same as in the summer. Before summer thunderstorms, everything goes still and silent, and there is a sort of tension in the air that's entirely different from the humidity. Something is coming, and everyone feels it.

The rain is then a break from the heat, a relief that saves crops and quenches the thirst of the dusty ground. In the winter, the rain doesn't benefit any crops and simply turns the ground cold and muddy. The air doesn't get still but is stirred up by howling gales. I feel a pre-rainstorm wind start up and am glad that I will be home when the storm breaks.

I turn onto the road that leads up the hill to the house I live in, a Victorian mansion built by cotton money that peers down, vulture-like, at the smaller frame houses surrounding it. I have to force my feet to keep moving. The only good thing about getting out at normal time from my job at the café is that I don't have to see my parents when I get home. But for some reason tonight Baby Grace, the owner of Sunnyside and anywhere from sixty to seventy years out of babyhood, has let me go early.

The closer I draw to my own house, the more a sense of oppressive unease descends on me. It's way too big for three people and always has been, and unlike with some families I know, there's no energy or enthusiasm of love to fill that great space.

I think when I was very young indeed my parents might have loved each other. I remember watching from the shag-carpeted floor of our living room, the only furnished room in the great big house my father had bought for a song and entered, tools in hand, to begin what he called fixing up and what most people called salvaging the grand old structure, watching as my mother spooned with my father in an ugly orange loveseat, her fair head against his dark one, briefly kissing him on the lips as I pushed Matchbox cars through the shag pile and heard him call her Sugarplum like the fairy, and somewhere in that memory is the sound of dishes clanking in the kitchen and a faint tune drifting through the unneeded butler's pantry so there must have been someone else in the house and it must have been Grandma.

When most people get home from work, they probably relax and take it easy, but when I get home I tense up even more. It's not just the piles of schoolwork that I know I have waiting for me, but the pressure of expectations.

I know there's got to be something that still keeps my parents together. And I know just as surely that

that something is me. I know full well the feeling of being adored by both parents, the way anyone with siblings imagines an only child must be. The thing is that although I've been adored by both parents, it has always been separately. I often feel that I would trade in that attention, that burdensome love, for exasperation and affection from both parents shared with any number of siblings. Then I would feel not only that I was less responsible, but that somehow the love I did get was truer.

But right now, I can tell that the only love my parents feel is toward me. Since Grandma died when I was six, I've been the only thing either one of them cares for, and in those years I've become cracked and strained like a rubber band that's been stretched around a sheaf of papers for too long. If I am the bond holding our family together, what will happen if I give out?

My mother's voice from the darkened living room one of the nights when I got home from the late shift at the motel calls out "Jerry? Jerry, is that you?" and then I know that I'll see her stretched out on the fancy plush sofa no more orange loveseat and I don't want to go to her don't want to make any noise. I want to run upstairs and tell Dad that this is his responsibility, this is his problem, this is his wife, goddamn it, and why doesn't he come here and take the bottle of scotch away and tell her that her brother isn't here and isn't ever going to be back here because he ran away from her and her goddamn crazy father just like she did, but instead I turn on the lamp on the table next to her and she squints in the darkness, eyes smudged with mascara, fumbling with a heavy clip-on earring and the jewelry that she's put on for no reason and stares at my face as though she's never seen me before.

"Paul, honey, is that you?"

"Yeah, Mom."

"What're you doing ... up so late?"

"The motel, Mom. My job at Frankie's."

Her unfocused eyes peer into mine and I take her wrist and try gently to coax her to get up but she snatches it away, offended and suspicious as a child, rubbing it and glaring at me.

"Don't touch me," she says. Okay I won't but why don't you just get up to bed it's late? "Paul, you need to go to bed. Here, let me help you." Okay Mom, why don't you do that. She smiles and stands and sways and I reach out to catch her and she leans heavily on me, staggering out of the room while muttering at me the whole time.

"Where's Jerry? Why hasn't he come home yet I could swear he would be back by now Daddy will be so mad Paul will you see to him when he comes in he might want a drink and then offer him your room you've got the nicest view across the river and everything should be perfect for Jerry when he comes back."

The words rush over me in a tide and at least she knows tonight that I am me and not Jerry, not the brother she hasn't seen since she was thirteen.

Laying a hand on my face and running her finger along my jawline she says, "You're a good boy. I know you are. I will always be able to count on you."

2

When I got my acceptance letter and scholarship to LSU, I was afraid my mother would cry. Her face fell, and I knew what I had suspected all along—that she didn't want me to go at all. I was her life, and if I left her here alone with my father, she would have nothing left to live for.

"Just get out!" My father was never so angry and his usually patient face was contorted with grief and rage. I stepped back, only thirteen years old far too young for any of this but too old not to understand what was going on.

I could see past the door he was trying to close, see the scene he was trying to block with his body, see my mother's reaching arms bobbing in and out of view her hands covered in blood and outstretched like the beggars in New Orleans the few times I'd been there. Her hands worked themselves into fists and then relaxed again and it kept the blood flowing, pumping from her arteries over her arms and as my father gave up and rushed past my horrorstruck form to the telephone she saw me and I swear she smiled even though she had been grimacing in pain.

I swear she smiled at me and tried to gesture for me to come near but that's when I ran from the vision worse than any I had seen on the ten o'clock "Horror Showcase" on Channel Ten, that's when I ran out the door and down the path and in my haste nearly off the cliff beside the river and I leaned over and vomited in the sweet spring grass while bees buzzed around me and the white crepe myrtle blooms fell over my head and I sobbed dry wracking sobs and vomited again so that the acrid smell covered up the scent of the nearby clover which only a few years ago Sissy Perkins and I had woven into clumsy chains for Mother's Day.

My father, in contrast, was immensely proud of my scholarship. He slipped me twenty bucks, a rarity for him, and told me to take out my favorite girl and do whatever I wanted. I didn't have the heart to tell him that girls around here find me more than a little odd. My dad doesn't know me very well, really. He admires my intelligence but does not want me to have an easy time in life. He believes work builds character. He also has a poor-man-turned-rich habit of hoarding, and sometimes hiding, his money to make sure that if the dream ends, he will not be left completely broke, the way he started out in life.

And so I hold the two jobs to pay what the LSU scholarship will not cover, hoping that by August I will have scraped together enough money and that my grades will not have slipped so much that I lose the scholarship.

Keeping up with work isn't easy when, four days a week, I drag myself home after one in the morning, then get up at five to finish my homework. I tell myself that I don't have to do as well as I'm used to, that the worst part is over now, but something in me just keeps pushing. It's not hard to make A's at my school, and I don't want to have my last semester there be a bust, even though I know they would still graduate me with honors. Call it pride, call it ambition, call it stupidity, but whatever it is, the two jobs have kept me working to the point of exhaustion every day.

3

My eyes itch and burn with tiredness, because even when I'm done with my work and done with my jobs, I hardly ever sleep. I sit up by the window and watch the sunrise over the river and check in on my parents and see that they too have lived for another day and maybe then I can doze off until my alarm shrills and I have to go subject myself to another day of school, not that it's awful but I do stick out a little.

I guess that was why Baby Grace let me go early today. I'd had a ten-page paper due earlier, and I'd risen at three a.m. to write it and have it ready to hand in by eight that morning. I'd caught a nap at the slow time in the motel, when Michael Predmore was there to cover for me if something happened. But by ten-thirty I was falling asleep over the cash register. The numbers kept blurring into one and after I'd rung up the same order incorrectly twice in a row, Baby Grace pushed me aside and directed me home.

"I've still got three hours here," I said stupidly.

"Not if you're working like that you don't!" she snapped back. Then, more softly, she added, "You look like my boys did when they needed their afternoon naps. You need more than a nap, Paul, or you're going to wear yourself old before your time. Go on home, college boy. I managed without you for thirty years, and I expect I can do it again for a night."

It's the nights that are always dangerous and that can seem never-ending, especially in the days before I took jobs that ended late. It was because of those endless nights and what I saw that spring day when I was thirteen that I first took up a razor, not to shave the fluff just beginning to show on my cheeks, but to cut, shallow at first, but sometimes deeper and harder and longer, until I could sleep.

That blood-letting, that release of pain, for me was the only thing that would end the long march through the loneliest hours of the night when even with my parents breathing in their twin beds in the next room I felt like I was the only one alive in the entire world.

And so I cut.

Another girly habit, like my care for classes and my manners and my refusal to get blind drunk at every opportunity. If anyone knew what I did in the desolate hours of the night, they'd probably call me a faggot like all the other times when I didn't want to fuck some girl in the back of my car or in the woods behind the school for cheap thrills and likely be married by the time I was eighteen, because I wanted out of this goddamn town and didn't want a kid or even a girlfriend to tie me down or notice the thin slice marks parading up and down my arms and the white lines of scar tissue that never tan, no matter how much time I spend outside in the blistering summers.

4

As I walk along now, drawing ever closer to my house, kicking up the cold dirt that will soon be splattered with rain, I'm not thinking about college or my parents and the silence that sits in our house, heavier than the air of summer thunderstorms, nor of my job in the café and why Baby Grace has chosen to be kind this particular night. I think, instead, about my job at the motel and about Casey, the girl I met there.

I don't think of Casey very often anymore, and why I ever thought of her as much as I did, I couldn't tell you. She wasn't the first girl that ever liked me. I've been told time and again that despite my skinny frame and too-large nose, I'm quite attractive. Sissy Perkins has had a crush on me for well over five years now, ever since that day in the spring when we were thirteen.

It's not that I don't like girls. My mind has run along the same track as nearly every adolescent boy's since the onslaught of puberty. It's just that I've always felt older than kids my age. Maybe it was the obligation I felt to my father, maybe it was a consequence of being an only child, or maybe it was that I did not feel free to depend on anyone, even my parents, and so had felt like an adult ever since I could remember.

My stomach and chest felt empty and I had nothing more to vomit up when Sissy found me beside the cliff. All of us neighborhood kids used to go there to play, and now it was kind of a meeting place for smoking and hasty sloppy make-out sessions. I should have chosen a better spot to try to be alone but maybe I even half-wanted someone to find me there and Sissy did, stepping gingerly around the pools of vomit in the grass and so quietly that I didn't even hear her until she sat beside me with a soft rustle and I looked at her, hastily rubbing my hands across my eyes and wiping my mouth, suddenly aware that my breath must smell rank and disgusting.

I just did not see the point in casually dating all the girls who had a fleeting interest in me. Sure, the hormonal side of me thought it was a brilliant idea, I could really have used a bit more action than I could give myself, but the few times I went out with anyone, and the even fewer times they attempted to kiss me, I pulled away.

I did not see any of these relationships heading anywhere, and so I did not feel as though I should lead on the girl I was with. True, they probably did not expect it to go anywhere except for the backseat of my Bronco, but for my own sake, even more than for theirs, I refrained. I felt I owed myself better.

Her eyes met mine and she looked so sad that I knew that she knew though I didn't know, then all of a sudden a stab of panic shot through me, making me feel as if my stomach had fallen to my feet, because what if she had come to tell me that my mother was dead? I didn't know if I could deal with that, because the only person I'd ever known who had died had been Grandma and I was so young then that I barely even understood what it meant much less how lonely it left my father.

She put her arm around me and I could not move. I could not decide if the actions she was taking were the sort that she would perform if she were going to tell me bad news so I stared into her round slightly chubby-cheeked face and noticed that she also had tears in her eyes, which almost convinced me until she laid her head on my shoulder and said, "Dad's gone."

The gears in my mind ground almost audibly as I tried to put together my father standing in the doorway and yelling at me with him leaving and then I thought maybe she meant for the hospital but mostly I was just relieved that my mother was still alive and then my thoughts stumbled and halted as I figured out that she meant her father not mine and that she didn't know anything at all about why I was there. So I awkwardly put my arm around her and tried not to breathe into her face and said nothing about why I was here why I was crying why I had puked because she didn't need that right now.

"What's wrong?" she asked, her voice muffled by my shoulder. "Why were you up here?"

And I never for a moment thought of actually telling her what was wrong, because it would mean trusting and the only person I'd been able to trust since I was very young was me and besides what right did I have to dump all my problems on her?

So I just said, "Some stuff" and would have shrugged except that her head was still on my shoulder and I was feeling very awkward and uncomfortable and all of a sudden she was crying and I was even more uncomfortable, especially since I could still feel that itchy heat behind my eyes that meant yet more tears were hiding there and I kept my eyes wide open so that the tears wouldn't fall but they leaked out anyway and I had cried so much that it was actually painful.

5

Now that I was almost out of here though, I was wondering whether I'd been wrong. Second-guessing myself is not something I do often, but I suppose a certain amount of nostalgia and reflection always comes as high school graduation approaches. I would never get misty-eyed recalling the overcrowded temporary classrooms encroaching on the derelict schoolyard we'd been packed into more and more often, or the raucous jeers that a teacher who tried to make students appreciate the subject was likely to get. But lately it was occurring to me more and more often that I had spent almost all of my life being desperately lonely. And as I thought about it, I began to fear that it was not merely a result of my situation, my school, my parents, but of me.

Would I still be shut off from everyone in college?

Finally, at last, I gave up and leaned my head against Sissy's and she didn't ask what was wrong again but we held each other and rocked together and it was a lot less awkward than any preteen petting session would have been, because we weren't there for release or escape, we were there to feel and to feel together that no matter how bad the reality was we couldn't ignore it anymore.

We finished together like should happen with sex and were left exhaling sharply into each other's shoulders and when we pulled apart I wiped her face and she wiped mine, just like when we were really little kids and we'd play in the fields and get pollen on our faces and wipe each other's off because we couldn't see our own, and I hooked my arm around my knee and stared off at the river and watched a slow-moving barge and she did the same and then she said, "Maybe someday we'll understand why."

Looking off over the river at the town across from ours and imagining the town after that and after that and so on and on, I felt suddenly how very small I was and how very trivial anything that happened to me would be in the grand scheme of things. I felt isolated and shut off from everything, especially from Sissy who still thought there might be someone older and wiser to offer her explanations, something I hadn't believed for years and so I said, "I doubt that day will ever come" and retreated into the loneliness that held me then and had held me for years.

6

The last time I can remember being truly and unquestioningly happy, feeling both loving and loved, was when my grandma was still alive. My father's mother, the only grandparent I ever knew, lived with us for a very brief time when I was little. I didn't realize it then, but the reason she stayed with us was that she was close to dying of the cancer that ultimately killed her. She could no longer manage alone, and she wanted to see her only "grandbaby" as much as possible before she departed from the world.

I have only put this together in retrospect. Knowing my grandmother when she lived with us, you would have thought cancer and death were the farthest things from her mind, and perhaps they were. She was a good old-fashioned southern woman in the way I, as someone who grew up there, think of them. Not in the corset-wearing-*Gone-With-the-Wind*-sipping-mint-juleps-on-the-veranda kind of way, but in the way I saw in Baby Grace and the other old timers.

My grandma was an old-fashioned southern woman in the sense that she saw the whole world as something that, like one of her children, could be hollered at, brought in, made to wipe its feet and wash up, and then sent off to bed after a biscuit and a cup of hot chocolate.

She didn't balk at work or problems of great magnitude, but threw herself at them full-force. She, like all her contemporaries, never thought for an instant that women should work less than men, and certainly not that they did. It was a given that everyone in a household worked, and if someone didn't, that person was lazy—a horrible insult indicative of a condition even worse than being on welfare. She had foresight in plenty, but she did not let it cause her to question in detail every step she took. She knew that if you hesitated too long, any chances you had would be gone.

My grandmother swept into our house when I'd just turned five and swept out again before I was six. I didn't realize right away that she'd gone to the hospital and died there. I thought she'd only gone back to where she lived before. When she was living with us, our house was an entirely different place. Instead of the oppressive silence of my parents, alone even when in the same room, the house hummed with the vibrations of life as she cleaned, cooked, and amused me.

I can hear her laughing and humming to herself as she twirled around the kitchen in a secret dance that was known only to her and the women she'd grown up with and to which I'd never be able to learn the steps because she was moving so quickly at her work that I didn't even have time to take in what she was doing. She would sing folk songs telling sad stories of doomed lovers or the robber Jesse James and sometimes singing out lively spirituals which made me feel like there really must be something in the world to praise. But despite all her singing she would only sing my favorite when she was making shortbread cookies. Even so, I would always demand she sing "the shortbread song" and she would laugh and smile at me, and if the time was right and the cookie sheet was greased, she would tap her foot in time to the rhythm and sing

Mama's little baby loves shortenin', shortenin'
Mama's little baby loves shortenin' bread.
Two little children lyin' in bed, one of 'em sick, and the other 'most dead.
Called the doctor and doctor said, feed them children some shortenin' bread.

As she sang it her hands would flash, unwrapping butter and measuring sugar with a practiced eye, and by the time she had got through the chorus the second time, she would be feeding me soft and deliciously sweet nuggets of shortbread dough.

7

When my grandma failed to come back after leaving for the hospital, my father came into my bedroom and told me what had happened. I had had no experience of death, except for the bodies of the mice and birds our cat Penny sometimes brought home, and I could not then envision any connection between the bloody messes on our porch and my Grandma who sang as she cooked.

"She's gone, Paul."

"But she'll be back soon?"

"No, son, she won't. She's ... dead. She's passed away."

My father was not kneeling down to my height the way adults often do when they have bad news to impart to a child. He sat on my bed and held me in his lap, wrapping his arm around me and holding me close.

He looked down at my upturned face, his eyes filled with tears. I knew he was trying to make me understand something about my grandma, but I couldn't. I was too young, and all I could see was that my father was crying. My father who I'd never seen cry, even when he slammed his thumb in the door of our old Ford, and it was that more than the news he was telling me that scared me and made me cry. He then held me to his chest and rocked me, and for the first and only time in my life he and I cried together.

My father's eyes looked bottomless, and I know now that he had lost more than just his remaining parent. He had lost the only ties he had to the life he remembered, a life in which his family didn't have enough money for even cloth diapers, and the older kids often went without eating so the younger ones could, because they remembered how hard it had been for them as toddlers to go hungry.

He wouldn't hear anyone else singing the songs that had kept them warm when the unheated house would not or smell hot-water bread frying when the only food left was cornmeal and bacon grease.

That part of his life was closed now. He was now Jeffrey Andrews, head of a successful shipping company and owner of the largest house in the town. He was not Jeff, digging ditches to lay pipe, or Jeffy, savoring the moments with his mother like those I had enjoyed. The past would not exist anymore except in his memory.

When I was five, I could not know any of this. All I knew was what happened after Grandma's death.

The house got colder and quieter. My father did not speak, except when absolutely necessary, and even then, he did not drink. My mother appeared to take up the slack for him by beginning the day with a fortifying gulp of Jim Beam from a bottle she hid beneath the sink, the cabinet door still baby-latched to protect me from the poisons inside.

8

I felt my parents drift, knew that the only thing they had in common was me, and with some sort of bitter pleasure, I denied them that. I loved my parents, especially my father, but I could not stand to be a piece of driftwood floating endlessly between their two islands. I preferred to be an island of my own.

I come downstairs to find that my father has slept in his study again and that my mother has started off the day with a Bloody Mary, but instead of saying anything to either of them, I grab my backpack and head for the car, noticing that one of my cuts from last night has reopened and is soaking through my shirt, but it's too late to do anything, because I am certainly not going back inside.

Ever since my grandmother died, I have been lonely. I cover it up with work and school and friendly, chatty relationships, but I have been ceaselessly lonely. With the ferocity of early adolescence, I was firmly convinced that no one truly knew how I felt, that no one else in the world could possibly understand.

Until I saw the girl who was lonelier than I was.

9

She checked in with her family, and although she held a curly-headed blond toddler in her arms, she looked at me in a way that was both appraising and openly sexual. This did not, however, set my blood pumping, the way it would have for ninety-nine percent of other boys my age, which was sixteen at the time.

Instead, it caused a deep stab of sympathy in me. Although she was trying to look seductive, she could not succeed with her eyes. They were not downcast like those of a victim, but stared at me with a challenge. I recognized the challenge for what it was, because I presented that same challenge to people who looked at me.

She was outwardly flirting, but inwardly she was daring me to find anyone—anyone at all—whose loneliness compared to hers.

I knew I could.

I registered that she was attractive, although too much makeup and a set of poorly punched holes in her ears detracted from her appeal. Yet it was not her looks, but my response to her challenge that made me ask her out that night. That was something I had never done before, ask a girl out. I'd had people set me up and had girls ask me, but this time I asked her. She seemed to know that I would, even though she could not possibly have known why.

The family headed away from the desk, and I took the opportunity to look at each one of them in turn. There were two other girls, the older one leading the younger by the hand. The older girl was maybe twelve or thirteen, and although her curves were softer and more noticeable than those of the lonely girl, she made no effort to display them. She walked stiffly and did not smile, even when talking with her younger sister.

The sister was much younger, maybe five, may six—it's hard to tell at that age—and had a mane of red hair that flowed out behind her. She skipped along beside her older sister, then suddenly stopped and turned her head to look back at me.

I gave a small wave, and she hid her face bashfully in the crook of her sister's arm. Then she looked up at the older girl and whispered something. The older girl also looked at me, but this time I did not wave. The fierce expression on her face had frightened me out of it.

As though he had noticed her look, and he probably had, the older brother looked at me too, and the girl's scowl was nothing compared to his. I looked away hurriedly and shifted some papers on the desk, but when I looked up, he was still glaring at me.

He had fallen behind the rest, and I had a sudden and probably not unfounded fear that he was going to come punch me in the face. He could do it, too. He was skinny as anything, but I could tell he was much stronger than I was.

He was also dashingly handsome, and I was sure if he had wanted to, he could have found more than a few willing girls in town. His hair was very dark and slightly wavy and flopped into his face from the center part. His eyes were a sorrowful deep brown. His features were delicate, but somehow this failed to diminish the tough-guy aura surrounding him.

I was scared of him, and I felt relieved as the lonely girl doubled back and touched his arm. As some unspoken understanding passed between them, he dropped his anger like a brick, and she smiled at him.

Bringing up the rear of the party was a slip of a woman I had not noticed. Her eyes were downcast in a way that told me she was used to going unnoticed, and if I hadn't already seen that there was no older man with them, I would have thought she was a battered wife, even though she had no visible bruises.

The thought still occurred to me as I took in her skittish gestures and nervous glances. Of course, maybe they were all running away from her abuser. But I saw nothing to support this beyond her behavior and nothing in the children to suggest they were runaways. The younger ones even looked happy.

The woman gazed at me for a moment, and in her blue eyes I glimpsed a ghost of what I had seen in her daughter's—appraisal, predatory lust, both crushed by the dead weight of isolation. The look was there for only a second, and then she turned away and followed after the children. She was shorter than the older ones—or maybe that was an illusion

produced by the way she was walking, hunched over
and drawn into herself, as if trying to disappear.

10

I watched until they had all gone up the stairs
leading to the outside corridor along which the rooms
are located. The motel didn't get much business, but
it got all the business there was. If you couldn't stay
with friends or relatives and wanted to sleep in a
room, you had to stay in the motel.

I busied myself with the endless paperwork that
motels require, filing rate cards, reserving rooms,
and preparing bills. I was concentrating on double-
checking the account book as a favor to Ned, the
purchasing agent, who had never been good at math
and wanted my assurance that his weekly report
wouldn't put his job in jeopardy. I had my head down
and was concentrating on entering Ned's figures in
the motel's primitive calculator, when the girl's voice
startled me so badly that I jumped and almost yelled
out loud.

*"That little wrinkle you get between your eyebrows
is very cute."*

*I look up, a bit panicked, and see her face less
than a foot from mine. I hadn't heard her come down.
She must have learned at some time how to move
like a cat. She leans languidly against the counter,
elbows resting on its scarred varnished wood. She
fumbles open the top two buttons on her plaid shirt*

232

so that I have a perfect view of her cleavage. She tosses her hair and leans in even closer, her breath smelling of stale cigarettes and Juicy Fruit gum.

"Cat got your ... tongue?"

Her voice is silky, and she licks her lips, then draws out the final word, as though it has an especially good flavor. When she tossed her hair, a few strands got caught in the gloss on her lips. They spoil the moist and inviting effect she must have been going for, and without thinking, I reach across the counter and brush them away.

She draws back, shocked, as if my fingers had radiated white-hot heat. But she recovered at once and gave a throaty, fake laugh.

"You're quicker than I thought. Without speaking one word to me, you get cutesy."

"Your hair was stuck in your lip gloss," I say quietly. I look directly into her eyes, and I see that I have rattled her again.

This time she tries a pouty anger.

"So now you want to be my makeup artist? Funny, when I don't even know your name."

"Paul."

"Just Paul? Like Cher?"

"Paul Andrews," I tell her, suddenly feeling pissed off. "Paul Christopher Andrews, sixteen, five-eleven, 128 pounds. I reside at 559 Coral Bell Road, and I drive a green 1986 Ford Bronco, license plate JAX 204. Do you need more information?"

I don't know what triggered this angry outburst. I decide that the hot fury I feel, transmuted into cold sarcasm, is because she seems to be denying the look

I saw in her eyes. Her flirting, her sexual banter are lies, and it upsets me that she would pretend she did not see the same loneliness in me.

To my surprise, she immediately drops the pretense.

"I'm Casey, short for Cassandra. My dad's idea." She sort of smiles. "Cassandra Margaret Camden. I'm also sixteen, but I don't reside anywhere anymore."

She picks up the pretense again, just as quickly as she had dropped it, and she extends her hand toward me with a flirtatious smile. I shake it, feeling the warm dampness of her fingers, satisfied now that I have seen through her façade and was not mistaken about her. She holds onto my hand, turns it over and examines it.

"Calluses," she says, raising her eyes to mine.

"Almost everyone around here has them."

"Almost everyone did where I'm from too."

She drops my hand, and I sense that she has again dropped her pretenses. She brushes back her hair, and the gesture is more practical than flirtatious.

"Where are you from?" I ask.

"Room 309," she says in a flat voice. "You should know, you checked us in."

"Shouldn't you be there with your family?"

I hope that she'll say something about them. Where's the dad? Why does the mom look so scared? How often does she do this kind of flirting? Is that the reason for the glares from the brother?

"Yeah, they wouldn't like me being down here. They think I'm feeding the ducks with my younger brother."

"Where's your brother?"

"Feeding the ducks." She stares at me, waiting. But I'm not sure for what exactly.

I look back and nod, without saying anything.

She looks disgusted, then turns and heads toward the front door, presumably to pick up her brother.

I call after her, "Casey!"

She whirls, expectant now. I give her what I guess she anticipates, but not for the reason she expects it. I hope that maybe in another setting I can draw her out. That we can join up, share something, prove that the connection I sense isn't all in my imagination.

"Want to do something later tonight?"

She smiles the practiced smile I noticed earlier, and I wish it had been the real one that I glimpsed.

"Can you do it late?" She cocks her head to one side, looking hopeful.

"This is my late night at the desk. Want to meet me in the lobby around midnight?"

"Okay."

She flashes the smile again and is gone with a toss of the hair. She's a good actor. She'd fool anyone. Well, anyone who wanted to be fooled. But I have never wanted that. I want reality, no matter how much it hurts. Better to know a world for something as bitter as it is than to be immersed in pointless fantasies.

Whenever I recall that night, I like to stop at the point when she smiles and walks toward the door. I'm tempted to now, because I know my house is just ahead of me.

Instead of going right to it, I veer off the road and onto a path beaten through the tall grass of an empty field. I want to have more time here, in the dark and away from the oppressive atmosphere of my house. I should get home before the storm hits, and for a moment I consider turning back, but I don't. I follow the path toward the river. After a few minutes, it comes into sight, and I see a fishing boat propelling itself upstream, its engines making a steady chugging sound. The white lights in its rigging give it a magical appearance as it glides over the dark water.

I think back to that night in the car.

11

She comes downstairs and is smoking.

The wafting smoke from her cigarette makes a cloud around her head in the blue-tinted florescent lighting of the motel porch. Her features are obscured by makeup, thick black mascara on her lashes so that her eyes look even hollower than before. Despite her short cutoffs and low-cut tank top, my eyes are drawn to her face where I see my own feelings registering there, feelings I have never detected in another person.

She looks rattled and I think that maybe later I will find out why. Right now I decide it is best not to say anything, to let her regain her composure and feel more comfortable. So we set out in my car for what I hope will be the beginning of the night that I stop feeling so alone.

12

It didn't work out like that.

We drove to the river and watched a fishing boat like the one I just saw. When she asked me if I wanted to talk, I thought she had the same idea that I did. I was so happy, so relieved that she was here for the same thing I was.

And then she tried to kiss me.

I probably could have reacted better, could have thought of something better to say, but my mind was reeling. Not only were my sixteen-year-old hormones fighting ceaselessly against my better judgment, but I couldn't tell what she was expecting.

"You're a virgin aren't you?" she asked.

God, yes, do you think I could bring myself to open up that way and show not just my body with its cuts and bruises and always-reopening wounds but any of myself to some girl from my school who would giggle away my serious questions and probably would just be dating me on a dare "Hey Deb, why don't you find out if Paul's really gay?"

When she went quiet again, I thought maybe we were getting the same idea. I don't know why I didn't come right on out and say that I'd thought we could really talk, but I think I still wanted her to get the idea herself. I didn't want to admit that I had been wrong thinking what I did about her, even though it was looking more and more like I had been.

"Sex is impersonal, an escape," she says.

Not for me although of course the sixteen-year-old boy part of me wants to just go ahead and fuck her brains out, after all she's giving me permission to do it, it's what she expects.

But somehow that makes it all the worse and I don't want to be her escape, don't want to be her distraction, I want to know her. I try to tell her this but she draws away from me not just physically but in every way possible, huddling against her side of the car.

"You should keep away," she says. "I'm a bitch. Me and my whole family have got one big fucked-up life that we share, and you shouldn't want in on it. I wouldn't want to blight your happy personal world."

My happy personal world.

My ... happy ... personal ... world.

Each word echoes in my head, and suddenly I see red—red like the flowers in the field where Sissy and I mourned together, red like the shag carpet I pushed toy cars through while my parents still loved each other, red like the blood on my mother's outstretched hands and like my own blood pouring over my cruelly sliced skin dotting the bathroom tile. And one of those drops becomes the whole world to me, my whole world in which I live alone and have to keep living alone. It was so stupid to try to share it with anyone. Now I've learned my lesson.

Now I really must stop remembering.

From age five on, I had decided to block people from my life. I had decided to shut my parents out the way they had shut out each other and not to give any girl the opportunity to put me in a relationship like theirs. I was smart, I was hard working, and I did not need people. Then this girl came along, and for once I found myself not wanting to be closed off, but to share, to share everything, because I felt that she would understand.

I shouldn't have been so careless. Even though I had told her nothing about me except a brief hint that my life wasn't all smiles and roses, I felt like I had let her in too far. But I had no way to know that she wasn't ready.

I dropped her off and went home.

13

My mother had fallen asleep in front of the TV again. I switched it off and covered her gently. My father sat in his study with a calculator on the desk in front of him. He nodded to me as I passed, and I raised a hand. I then stretched out on my bed and cried, hating myself for it.

I don't sob or snuffle. I just let the tears slip out as they wanted to when I was in the car. I sometimes feel like there's nothing inside me but tears because I feel so empty and this is the only thing that ever comes out. The tears and the blood are the only ways I know that I am still alive.

I need something else. I need her.

She may not be ready now, but I am more than ready to be saved from this emptiness, to be saved from myself. That's why, when I check them all out the next day, I hand her a slip of paper with my name and address.

She gives me a surprised, searching look. Not taking her eyes off mine, she folds the paper and puts it in her purse. Then without a word, she is gone. I feel hope surge in my chest. She didn't throw it out. And the look she gave me had no pretenses.

Perhaps she is closer than I knew.

14

Nearly three years have passed since I watched her walk out of the front door of the motel, and I have heard nothing from her.

I wonder if she long ago threw out the paper with my address or lost it. Maybe she doesn't remember me or maybe it's something else I can't imagine. I like to think it was something else, something beyond her control.

I remembered the way she had said in a hollow voice, "I don't reside anywhere anymore," and I thought that maybe my giving her my address might make her think I was mocking her or insulting her.

I thought maybe she had been killed in a car crash. I even thought, at my craziest, that maybe she had become an actress in Hollywood.

I've wondered a lot of things about her, and I continue to do it as I sit by the river remembering the brief time we were together. I'm starting to feel something that I've known on some level all along, coming to some understanding that is prompted by recalling my night with Casey.

I'm beginning to understand that all those years ago, I forced myself unnecessarily into loneliness, that I was afraid I would be as useless and disappointing to others as they had been to me. I was afraid, I suppose, of my own failure, even before it happened.

Remembering Casey's words and how they crushed me brings that fear to the surface again, but this time I hold it there. I want to get used to it, to confront it. After all, it is a part of me, it is reality, and I must face that.

After about twenty minutes, I am so cold that the only thing I'm afraid of anymore is pneumonia. So I turn back and walk much more quickly toward my house.

The storm is now on the verge of breaking full force, and I swap my striding for running as my house looms on the horizon. I pound up the hill enjoying the burning in my lungs and calves. It makes me feel more concretely alive than all the thinking that I did. I reach the overhang of the front porch just as the first fat drops of rain hit the dirt.

I stand on the porch and watch as the deluge begins. Rain pours off the roof in sheets and rushes through the downspout with a gurgling sound. Lightning flashes, bathing my car in the driveway with an ethereal white light for a brief moment, then thunder cracks and booms directly overhead, shaking the house and making the porch light blink.

Shivering with cold, I retreat inside and shut the door. The house is still and quiet, and, as another clap of thunder sounds, the lights go out. The hum of the refrigerator also stops, and I say *Damn* under my breath, thinking of the food that is likely to spoil. I put my hand on the radiator nearest me and find that it is still warm. I remember that they don't go out with the power, and I'm comforted by that. It might be dark, but at least it will be dark and warm, not dark and cold.

The idea of fixing myself a snack in the dark discourages me from trying; I find the newel post by groping, then make my way upstairs by feel. My parents have to be asleep or they would be out in the hall, my dad reassuring my mother that everything would be all right.

I feel my way along the wall and go into my room. I remember that I have a flashlight in the drawer of the bedside table, and just hope that its batteries aren't dead.

I switch on the flashlight, and to my relief, its light is strong and bright. I lay it down on my bed, and by its light, I get undressed and pull on my pajamas. I decide that I can skip brushing my teeth until morning.

I've just climbed between my cold sheets when I hear the noise. At first I think it must be more thunder, but I realize that it is far too regular and, furthermore, it just keeps going on.

I decide that a window or door must have blown open and is now banging in the wind. In an old house like ours, incidents like that aren't unusual. I am tempted to ignore it, because I'm just getting comfortable in my bed. Instead, I pick up the flashlight and creep downstairs, trying not to wake up my parents.

I'm all the way downstairs before I realize that the sound isn't the bumping of a loose window sash, but someone knocking on the front door.

My heart starts pounding.

A knock this time of night in our town means nothing but trouble. Some kids have been swept away in the river, a toddler is missing, a neighbor has had an accident or a heart attack and needs a ride to the hospital or, worse, somebody has died.

The only other time I can recall someone pounding on our door so late was when Sissy came to say that old Doc Armstrong had collapsed while tending to her mother, who had a high fever and was experiencing severe right-side pains. Both needed to be taken to the hospital, and Sissy had been sent to ask my dad for help.

Hoping I wasn't going to face anything worse than that, I took a deep breath and pulled open the door.

15

I shine my flashlight on the figure standing there. I'm stunned and puzzled for what seems like a full minute. Finally my brain registers what—who—I am seeing.

Casey!

She's obviously soaked to the skin, even though she seems to be wearing several layers of clothes, maybe all she owns. Her hair is longer than when I last saw her, and far from being a sleek mane, it's plastered around her face, which is white with cold. Her eyes are wide, as if she is as surprised to see me as I am to find her standing on my front porch.

Before I can speak, she hurls herself at me, knocking the flashlight out of my hand, and hugging me with such force that for a moment I can hardly breathe. But then I respond, pulling her against me as if I'm trying to weld our bodies together. Her wet clothes soak my pajamas, but I hardly notice.

"Paul," she says, almost gasping my name. "I knew you would be here. I just knew you would!"

Her head is resting against my chest, and she begins to talk, almost as if to herself. Blood is pounding in my ears, and I can't make out what she says. For a moment, I wonder if I am only having a realistic dream. Three years of nothing, then she turns up and knocks on my door.

She pulls away from my hug and takes a step backward.

"You really are Paul, aren't you?" She sounds alarmed. "Paul Andrews?"

"Of course I am." I pick up the flashlight and point it toward myself. "And I know who you are, but your turning up at my house after all these years is just a little ... strange," I finish lamely.

What I have just said suddenly strikes me as absurd. I grin, then I begin to laugh. I try to stop, because Casey will think I've gone crazy, but the word strange doesn't come close to capturing the situation.

Then Casey starts to laugh too.

I take her arm and guide her inside, out of the cold. I shut the front door, and we both keep on laughing. We hug each other, and then finally fall silent.

"Hungry?" I ask.

"Starving," she says.

I lead her into the living room and guide her to one of the large leather club chairs in front of the fireplace. I wrap her up in the patchwork quilt my grandmother made that is draped over the back of the chair. It takes only a moment to light the gas logs in the fireplace, and the yellow and blue flames instantly chase away the dark and fill the room with a warm glow.

"Stay here and warm up," I tell Casey. "I'll be back with something to eat in just a minute."

She smiles and nods and her whole body under the quilt seems to relax.

I put the flashlight on the windowsill in the kitchen and get a package of sliced cheddar and a jar of mustard out of the refrigerator. The light in the refrigerator is out, of course, so I have to fumble around to locate the cheese. The bread is in the bread drawer, and while I'm fixing a sandwich for Casey, I realize that I'm also hungry. I make two sandwiches, put them on plates, and get out two paper napkins. I add two glasses of water to the tray.

I'm about to take the sandwiches into the living room when I realize that we have ice cream in the freezer. With the power out, it's sure to melt, so I take out the two pints and put them on the tray with the sandwiches. I almost forget spoons, but I don't.

Casey wolfs down her whole sandwich before I'm half finished with mine. She eats as if she hasn't eaten in days, and maybe she hasn't.

"That was really good," she says.

"Hope you have room for ice cream," I say, realizing too late how stupid that must sound to someone who seems to be starving. "Strawberry or chocolate?"

"Strawberry, definitely."

She takes the carton, pulls off the lid, then begins to eat the ice cream almost as fast as she had devoured the cheese sandwich. When she finishes, I pass her mine, mostly uneaten, and she tackles that too. I sit back in my chair opposite her and watch her.

Her face swims in the firelight, and I notice that she looks different. Her face is thinner, her cheekbones sharper, and her hair longer, but it's not the physical changes that I most notice.

The defiant, challenging look in her eyes that I had seen when we first met in the motel has gone. She looks up at me, and I wonder if she is noticing something similar about me. Have I lost what she likely considered an arrogant, judgmental look?

I realize that even after only a few minutes with her, I do not feel as lonely as I did by the river. Something has now clicked into place, the last piece of an exasperating jigsaw puzzle.

Or maybe what has clicked are the first two pieces

of a new puzzle, one that won't be so frustrating.

"I told you that night that our family was fucked up," she says. "And I'm glad you ... turned me down, because that eventually made me understand myself better. Understand what I really wanted and was missing."

"If that's what made you come here, I'm glad."

"My dad was a drunk who walked out on us, leaving my mother with six kids and no money." Her voice is soft, as if speaking to herself. "I think she went a little crazy, because for years, when we weren't staying with our grandma, she dragged us around looking for him."

She turns her head away. "She did what she had to do to earn money, but she was wild at heart. Drinking and taking drugs with the men she let pick her up was all part of the fun."

"That must have been hard." I know I sound lame, but I don't know what else to say.

"Particularly on Sarah and Jen, and Tommy, the littler kids," Casey says. "Mom would pull us out of school and go on the road, and Jen in particular loved school. And none of them—none of us—got to make friends we could keep."

I listen without interrupting her. I realize she wants me to get to know her, and that means getting to know her family. I can tell that will take hours and hours of talking over days and weeks, maybe months and years. Still, it's a beginning, and I welcome her willingness to let me into her life.

"Jared is the oldest, and for a long time he felt he had to try to take Dad's place." She shrugs slightly.

"I understood that, but he and I got into fights all the time, because he tried to make me do what he thought was right. Looking back, I can see he was right more often than I was."

"Did he stay with your family?"

"No, he left," she says. "He and Will, who was my second older brother, talked about what they should do, and they agreed that one of them had to get away. Otherwise, both of them would be suffocated by us and maybe end up as drunks like Dad."

"So Jared left because he was the oldest in the family?"

"No, he and Will played a game, and the one who won would be the one who left. Jared won, but Will told me that he felt he had won, because he wanted Jared to get away."

"So Will never tried to escape from the family?"

"Oh, no," she says. "That's not who he was. He tried to take Jared's place the way Jared had tried to take Dad's. He did his best to be the perfect son and the perfect brother."

"He's the one who gave me a threatening look when you were talking to me at the motel desk."

"That was him trying to make me behave the way he thought Jared would want me to." She falls silent for a moment. "He came up with the idea of killing himself to shock Mom out of her dream world and face the fact that our family was fading into nothingness. He knew that if she didn't come out of her craziness and stop chasing after Dad, the family would eventually fall apart. The littler kids would go into foster homes, and I'd end up working in a bar or worse."

"Will killed himself to shock your mother?" I'm confused and can hardly believe what I'm hearing. "Wasn't there some other way?"

"Will was the only thing in the world besides Dad that Mom cared about. I volunteered, but Will said Mom had given up on me as a worthless tramp, and of course, we couldn't sacrifice any of the littler kids."

"A terrible price," I say. "Did it pay off?"

"Everything worked out the way Will thought it would," she says. "Mom was a basket case. Because I was the oldest left, I took her and the little ones to Grandma's house in Mississippi. We eventually moved into our own house, and Sarah and Jen are back in school. Tommy is in kindergarten and has already learned to read."

"How about your mother?"

"She's better now, mostly because Jared came back home. While he was gone, he took courses at a community college in New York, and he plans to go to Jackson State and become a psychologist."

"A psychologist?"

"He says that because of his experiences, he has a better idea about how to help people get their lives together."

"Does your dad know about Will?"

"I don't know how he could." She pauses. "But I think it would almost kill him if he did."

"Even though he abandoned the family?" I'm surprised.

"I know he loved us and I'm sure he still does." Casey sounds wistful. "He just didn't know what to do with us and thought that he was helping us by leaving."

I find that puzzling, but I don't say anything.

"I still love him." Her voice is soft. "But it's really Will that saved us, and I love him even more. When I met you, I realized that you're like Will."

I don't interrupt her, but it seems to me that Will, with his hot temper and self-sacrificing love for his family, was the opposite of me. I'm more like Jared—quiet, reserved, and deeply lonely. I know this is not what Casey wants to hear, so I keep quiet.

She tells me about finally deciding to come find me, once she felt like the family was stable and could do without her. She didn't have enough money for a bus ticket, so she hitchhiked from Laurel, Mississippi.

"I never took a ride from a single guy," she says "That's too dangerous for a girl traveling alone. I waited at rest areas for families or couples or women."

"That was sensible."

I look at her face in the firelight and think that she looks younger, not older, than when we first met. Without the makeup and without the swagger, she now seems to be who she really always was.

That's why I kiss her.

The kiss is long and lingering and tastes of strawberry. She is the first girl I have kissed, and I don't know if I'm doing it right. But I don't care, because I'm wholly lost in the experience.

We pull apart, and I see the glint of tears on Casey's cheeks. I feel a moment of panic, fearing that I've done something wrong, then she reaches out from under the quilt and takes my hand. She squeezes it gently and looks up at me with moist eyes.

"I'm the first girl you ever kissed," she whispers.

I nod slightly, and she squeezes my hand tighter.

I take my hand away and wipe the tears from her cheeks with the flat of my thumb. She begins crying harder and shakes her head.

"What's wrong?" I ask, in a hushed tone.

She shakes her head again.

"Nothing," she says, her voice breaking. "Everything is right this time."

She pulls back the quilt, then as I move closer to her, she wraps it around us both. Her wet clothes are cold against the thin cotton of my pajamas. I slip an arm around her shoulders, and she cuddles up against me.

The storm has died down, but a steady stream of rain beats against the windows. The power is still off and probably won't be back on until morning. But the steady glow from the fire provides all the light and warmth we need.

"Can you sing?" Casey asks me out of nowhere.

"Like everybody else," I say. "But I'm no Elvis."

"My dad used to sing to me when I was upset. Will you sing something so that I can sleep now?"

I try to think of something that is low and comforting, but nothing occurs to me.

"Sing what?" I ask. "Anything in particular?"

"Anything at all," she says. "I just want to hear the sound of your voice."

All I can think of is my grandma and her work-worn hands that are surprisingly soft when she rests them on my small shoulders, then bends over and kisses the top of my head.

I begin to sing the song I always asked her for, but I sing it in a slow tempo, turning her lively dance tune into a gentle lullaby.

Mama's little baby loves shortenin', shortenin'
Mama's little baby loves shortenin' bread.
Put on the skillet. Put on the lid.
Mama's gonna make some shortenin' bread.
Mama's little baby loves shortenin', shortenin'
Mama's little baby loves shortenin' bread.
Two little children lyin' in bed, one of 'em sick and the other 'most dead.
Called the doctor and doctor said, feed them children some shortenin' bread.

Looking down at her face, I see that she is asleep, so I stop singing. I can only guess how exhausted she must be. I hold her close and watch her take deep, regular breaths and feel the warmth on my neck when she exhales.

When I hold my breath for a moment, I can feel her heartbeat. That is when I know that as ugly as reality can be sometimes, nothing can be more real or more beautiful than this.

I don't care what my parents will say when they wake up and find her in our living room. I don't care if she decides to go to college with me or not. I don't care if her family likes me or not.

For once, I don't want to escape from my life. For once, everything is right, and I don't ever want to leave.

About the author

Rebecca Grove Munson was born in 1984 and became a writer at the age of four, when she sat on her dad's lap and typed HI BIG PIG on the computer screen. This was followed by the dictated story *The Grocery Store Mystery*, which appeared in the *Wilson School Thistle* and so became her first publication. In the fourth grade, she started a newspaper, but she soon found that she preferred making up stories to reporting them.

During her many years of education, Rebecca always found time to write. At John Burroughs School in St. Louis, she was co-editor of *The World,* the student newspaper; an editor of the literary magazine, *The Review*; and a contributor to *The Governor,* the yearbook. In the ninth grade, she started her first novel, *The Winds of Time.* Encouraged by the responses of her friends, she continued working on it for the next three years. Rebecca's lyrics for the Christmas song "Frozen Teardrops Fall" were set to music by Stuart McIntosh and performed at her school and at other venues.

During summer breaks while in high school and college, Rebecca worked as a technician in a laboratory researching breast cancer at Washington University Medical School. She learned such esoteric skills as how to run a gel and perform a polymerase chain reaction. Her interest in science never overshadowed her interest in writing, and she continued to write stories during the summer, several of which appeared in online publications. Her story "Sometimes" was published in the July 2001 edition of *Young Writer Magazine* (London).

Rebecca graduated with Honors from Burroughs in 2002, and in 2006 she earned an A.B. from Columbia University. She graduated Magna Cum Laude and Phi Beta Kappa, with Departmental Honors in English. During her undergraduate years, she was Senior Staff Writer for the *Columbia Daily Spectator*. She founded and was later elected president of the Nobel Kinsmen, a group for the dramatic reading and discussion of Shakespeare. Under the tutelage of Arnold Weinstein, the librettist for the opera version of Arthur Miller's *A View from the Bridge*, she wrote her first dramatic scenes. But her real love was for narrative fiction, and before graduating, she finished the first draft of her novel *Someday Never Comes*.

Rebecca spent her next year at Keble College, Oxford, pursuing her interest in Shakespeare and early modern drama. As a member of the Middle Common Room, she made new friends and enjoyed the social and intellectual life of Oxford. She lived in college rooms, wore her gown to elaborate dinners, punted on the Isis, and drank at the Eagle and Child, the pub where J.R.R. Tolkien and C.S. Lewis met to discuss their stories. She lived the sort of Oxford life she had read about, but when she was not in lectures or out for fun, she was conducting research in her favorite location, the Duke Humphrey Library, a collection of manuscripts and books housed in the Bodleian Library. Fans of the Harry Potter movies, of which Rebecca was one, would immediately recognize the setting.

In 2007, Rebecca graduated and received a Master's degree with Distinction from Oxford. Continuing on the academic path, she next earned a Ph.D. with Honors from the University of California, Berkeley, in 2014. While a graduate student, her Shakespeare research was supported, in part, by grants from Harvard University, Yale University, and the Folger Shakespeare Library. In addition to teaching undergraduate courses and working on her dissertation, she completed the short novel *Jane Doe-22*, which was a contender for the Paris Literary Prize.

After graduating from Berkeley, Rebecca spent two years as a postdoctoral fellow, first at the University of California, Los Angeles, then at Emory University. She was an enthusiastic teacher, and at both institutions, in addition to doing her own research, she was able to teach courses that allowed her to draw on her deepening knowledge of literature.

At the end of her last fellowship, Rebecca joined the Center for Digital Humanities at Princeton University in a position that combined administration, research, and teaching. Eager to learn more about the new discipline, she returned to Oxford and earned a certificate in digital research. Soon after, she was promoted to become Assistant Director of the CDH. Pursuing her own research, she established a database of Shakespearean marginalia and presented papers on Shakespeare at the Folger Library and academic conferences.

In 2018, at the age of thirty-four, Rebecca was diagnosed with triple-negative metastatic breast cancer, the most aggressive form of the disease. Displaying steely determination and no hint of self-pity, she continued to work, teach, and write. Characteristically, she cofounded the online support group Young and Strong at Dana-Farber Cancer Center, where she was treated. She also began writing the blog *Pitiless Achilles Wept,* which chronicled her experiences with breast cancer.

Even after her diagnosis, Rebecca stayed in touch with her friends and continued to make new ones. Although the COVID pandemic was in full force, her friends came to her aid, accompanying her to chemotherapy sessions, doing her grocery shopping, or sometimes just having a socially distanced drink with her on her patio. Thanks to their kindness, she was saved from isolation.

That Rebecca was intelligent is obvious from her educational accomplishments, that she was beautiful can be seen from a glance at her photograph, that she was talented is clear from her writing. But her sharp wit, ready warmth, natural kindness, unbridled capacity for friendship, and iron-clad loyalty to those close to her can only be appreciated by those who knew her.

As an only child growing up, she treated her dogs almost as if they were siblings, and Cookie, Captain, Shadow, Skipper, and Scout all returned her love and demonstrations of affection. Yet during her last months, it was her cat Percy who supplied her with the immediate love and reassurance she had always valued in her animal friends.

Rebecca died in her childhood home in the early hours of August 13, 2021. That it was Friday the 13th would have amused her. Before going to sleep, she and her parents had watched an episode of *The Gilmore Girls*, one of her favorite shows. Her parents remained with her during the night.

The top of the Indiana limestone bench dedicated to Rebecca's memory at John Burroughs School reads

A flash of lightening . . .
Brilliant, Electrifying, Brief

Yet it is the inscription along the edge in words suggested by her friends that best captures the person Rebecca was

Kind Loving Funny Beautiful Talented
Loved By Her Friends Adored By Her Parents
And Her Dogs

At this point Rebecca might say: Bid the soldiers shoot.

www.ingramcontent.com/pod-product-compliance
Lightning Source LLC
Chambersburg PA
CBHW020652120726

47906CB00001B/242